James McCarroll

Madeline and other Poems

James McCarroll

Madeline and other Poems

ISBN/EAN: 9783741124907

Manufactured in Europe, USA, Canada, Australia, Japa

Cover: Foto ©Andreas Hilbeck / pixelio.de

Manufactured and distributed by brebook publishing software
(www.brebook.com)

James McCarroll

Madeline and other Poems

MADELINE

AND OTHER POEMS

BY

JAMES McCARROLL

WITH A PORTRAIT OF THE AUTHOR

AND AN INTRODUCTION BY

CHARLES LOTIN HILDRETH

———

CHICAGO, NEW YORK, & SAN FRANCISCO

BELFORD, CLARKE & COMPANY

PUBLISHERS   ·

LONDON: J. H. DRANE, PATERNOSTER ROW,

INTRODUCTION.

If to absorb through the spiritual senses all that is good and precious in our common life and the visible world about us and give it back in clear and tender music, is to be a poet, then James McCarroll, whose collected verse is here for the first time presented to the public, is one of the truest poets that ever touched the lyre of gold. His long and useful career has not been passed in the quiet gardens of the Academy, or in the seclusion of the scholar's cloister, but in the very market-place of life, among the busiest toilers of the world. From a very early age he has been connected with the press, and probably has the honorable distinction of having edited or been connected with more newspapers, journals, and magazines than any other man in America. Twenty years ago, the *Buffalo Courier* spoke of him as "the veteran editor." He was editor and proprietor of the *Peterborough Chronicle* in 1841, and many other papers still flourishing in various parts of the country owe their success, 'and, in not a few instances, their very existence, to his efforts. He was for many years surveyor of the port of Toronto, and has occupied other important public positions under the Canadian Government. While filling these positions, and in the course of his many public lectures and concert perform-ances—for he is a celebrated flautist and musician as well as a composer of rare talent—he made the acquaintance of a host of famous people, both in political life and in artistic circles ; among others, Jenny Lind, Lucca, Sir Jules Benedict, Vieuxtemps, Wieniawski, Ole Bull, Catherine Hayes, Maurice Strakosch, Arabella Goddard, Madam Anna Bishop, Herr Griebel, Carl Formes, etc. Not a few of these acquaintances ripened into lasting friendships, and many a one whose name the world delights to honor will recognize among the pieces comprised in this volume, songs sung or verses recited at social gatherings where the genial and witty poet was a central figure.

As a young girl sings at her daily task merely because the music within her heart overflows at her lips unaware, James McCarroll has written his poems in the midst of unceasing and, too often, uncongenial and vexatious occupation. Amid the thunder of the presses and the myriad-voiced confusion of public office life he has found a quiet place within himself, full of flowers and sunlight, the notes of birds and the murmur of streams, into which no jar or clamor of the world could enter, and where these tissues of song were woven into imperishable beauty. That he has not before brought these scattered sprays into one bouquet has not been from lack of the appreciation of others, but from the indifference with which so many makers of song regard their works when once completed and sent forth into the world.

James McCarroll's verse is essentially optimistic. That dark philosophy which sees in Beauty only the masked skull, and places in the hands of Time only the hour-glass and the scythe, has no place in his art. He has that happy faculty, which is denied to most of us whose eyes have grown purblind with tears shed over wasted hopes, vanished friendships, and the many wrongs of time, of seeing the world as a rose-garden, darkened, it may be, at intervals by brief April showers, but for the most part basking in the warm gold of unclouded sunshine. To him pain, sorrow, and misfortune are the accidents, not the essentials of existence. He feels that

> " An honest heart, and sturdy hand,
>   These are the implements we want—"

And with these most of the ills of life may be overcome, and those that are irremediable must be borne as well as may be. Sin is a misfortune to be pitied ; the cloak of charity is wide enough to cover all human failings.

> " Vice is but Virtue's poor prodigal son."

Only for the Pharisee praying loudly on the public street has he any contempt ; the poor publican, humbly conscious of his own weakness, is his brother, whom he gladly acknowledges.

What is rare, in these days at least, in an imaginative poet, he possesses a vein of keen and exquisite humor— he were no true countryman of Tom Moore's else. But his humor is of the kind that laughs, not sneers. There is hardly a line of satire in his whole work. And what is true of all real humor, within him the source of laughter lies close to the fount of tears.   The beggar's visage may be a ludicrous one, but his coat is old and his stomach is empty ; and if you laugh at him your hand goes to your pocket to share your scanty purse with a brother a little poorer than yourself.

But it is in such poems as "The First Bath," of which Oliver Wendell Holmes expressed his admiration in a letter, quoted in the appendix to this volume, that James McCarroll is at his best :

> " Once more God leans against the purple bars
> That close the rosy portals of the day;
> Till, slowly through a mist of fading stars,
> Before His shining shoulder they give way,
> And outward rolls His treasurer, the sun—"
> *   *   *   *   *   *
> ——" Wondrous changing webs of jewelled gauze
> From out His great, round coffers of the sea,
> Far up the heavens, with lustrous hand He draws."

In this humble tribute to the genius of my friend and colleague, I feel that I have fallen far short of that praise which is his right ; but I believe that his readers, those who have long known and loved his work and those who meet with it now for the first time, will not fail to understand and appreciate, as it deserves, the purity, humanity and beauty of this golden harvest of a well-spent life.

CHARLES LOTIN HILDRETH.

April, 1889.

CONTENTS.

MADELINE.

Beside a summer river that was flowing
Clear, cool and gently through a sunny vale,
As though it were a liquid west-wind blowing
A sort of luscious, lazy, silvery gale
Between two odorous banks with cowslips glowing
In knots of tangled gold, deep tinged and pale,
And morn-tipt daisies sprinkling brakes of wildwood,
The fairy haunts of memory, love and childhood,

There in a nook with wonderous beauty beaming—
A mine of woodland jewels lit with showers
That left the shaded dell with incense teeming
As though it were the passion time of flowers—
A nook where Autumn dozed in golden dreaming
And blue-eyed spring came in her first bright hours,
Tripping along to robin-red-breast measures,
Beneath a fragrant store of primrose treasures—

A sylvan temple on whose emerald altar
Sweet Nature spread her offerings to the sun,
While thrilled the raptures of her warbling psalter,
Not doling out her riches, one by one
With a spare hand that ever seemed to falter ;
But letting them in wild profusion run,
As though her lap were heaped with each rare token,
And on that spot her apron strings had broken.

Be patient ! In that dewy glimpse of Eden
Stood a sweet little gipsy of a cot,
White as a dove, low-eaved and woodbine laden,
A sort of thatch and stone, " forget-me-not "--
But first I should have spoken of the maiden,
The living charm—the bright, I don't know what—
Young Madeline, poor Lady Bertha's daughter,
The spirit of that grove and shining water—

Young Madeline who from each dazzling shoulder
Seemed ready to shake out a golden plume,
With which 'twere almost strange not to behold her,
Such nameless lustre mingled with her bloom ;
But, then, one other touch too bright would mould her
And seal the lovely incarnation's doom ;
For heaven would see where it o'erstepped its duty
And draw her back within its lines of beauty.—

Young Madeline that struck you with such wonder—
That laughed all fabled loveliness to scorn,
When e'er she drew her casement bars asunder
And waged her eye and cheek against the morn ;
The bright, ineffable, angelic blunder,
So strange it was that she was earthly born :
But yet, not strangest, for in her was given
The surest hostage of our claims on heaven.

Entranced and lost while on each feature dwelling,
And so bewildered by her radiant form,
The gazer felt description but mere spelling
Through the mysterious volume, soft and warm ;
Her lips, her throat, her snowy bosom swelling,
Her hair as dark as midnight in a storm,
Were all the sweetest, whitest, richest, rarest,
Till she was called "Young Madeline the fairest."

But there was one who studied those pure pages
With all the ardor of his heart and brain,
Who could have pondered o'er them through long ages,
And still enraptured turned to them again
To drink afresh the lore that tottering sages
With scanty locks declare to be in vain :
Young Edward, from Lord Harold's distant towers—
A minstrel of most courtly speech and powers.

'Twas on a balmy evening while decoying
The silvery tenants from that lovely stream,
And in the fulness of his youth enjoying
A sort of calm, delicious, waking dream,
That Madeline, at once the spell destroying,
Burst on his vision like a sudden beam :
She, too, by chance, along the banks was straying,
Listening to what the gentle tide was saying.

They glanced each at the other's matchless splendor,
She, at his godlike form and sculptured face,
He, at the wondrous charms that seemed to lend her
The last transcendent touch of earthly grace,
And in ethereal beauty heaven-ward send her ;
But instantly she hastened to retrace
The path to where her snow-white cot was gleaming,
And left him now, at least, securely dreaming.

With pallid cheek, next morn when day was dawning
She left her pillow that was sorely tossed,
And sat beneath the fragrant woodbine-awning,
In strange sad reveries, and silence lost ;
And, when poor Carlo came up to her fawning,
She said she'd pat him, but her sleep was cross'd
With dreams, that came in spite of all her wishes,
" Of naughty sportsmen, fishing rods, and fishes,"

The pulses of her inmost soul's devotion,
Unconsciously had just begun to play,
Like his who set them all in such wild motion,
And who again might never pass that way :
In truth, she launched out on so vast an ocean
That she sat dreaming through the live-long day,
Until once more at eve she sought the river
For the sweet calm its music used to give her.

'Twas fate ! young Edward soon was close beside her,
Though on her arm the lady Bertha hung,
And did with matron glances gently chide her
For the surprise that half escaped her tongue ;
But she had native modesty to guide her ;
And Edward's glance was on the waters flung ;
For he, of course, was quite absorbed in fishing ;
While she to see one caught was only wishing.

Soon o'er the waves, the silken line was tightening,
And suddenly, before the maiden's view,
The rod was arched, and up the stream like lightning
A shining creature in its terror flew,
Its ardent scales the purple waters brightening
As out they flashed in many a changing hue,
Until at last, it was securely lying
Upon the bank, among the cowslips, dying.

The youthful sportsman played his part so featly,
That lady Bertha covered him with praise ;
But soon she found she had not done discreetly ;
For Madeline's fair face was in a blaze,
At words that fell upon her ear so sweetly,
And left her trembling with averted gaze ;
"Till she, to hide the tale her cheek was telling,
Had almost turned alone towards her dwelling.

The fish, he was, in sooth, a royal fellow ;
His sides were argent, deepening into gold ;
And all be-dropt with crimson and with yellow
His emerald back blazed forth, a thousand fold.
His head was ruby-tinted, dark and mellow,
In truth, he was so glorious to behold,
That Madeline took courage from her mother,
And cried : " oh ! do, sir, try and catch another."

He bowed, and with some pleasant words, and smiling,
Again the line flew from the giddy reel ;
But this time, all in vain the fly's beguiling,
No fish approach its barbéd sting of steel ;
But though not dreaming of a touch defiling
Her flowing veil, before which he could kneel,
He, somehow flurried by the words she uttered,
Caught it as on the balmy breeze it fluttered,

She, laughing, clapped her hands in sportive wonder
Till her gemmed fingers into lightning flashed,
Because that he should make so queer a blunder,
And stand before her pleading and abashed ;
But soon he pinched the veil and hook asunder,
And his lithe rod into the current dashed ;
But as the gauze back to her shoulders dangled,
She wished it had not been so slightly tangled.

That eve, young Madeline heard fond words spoken,
Such as till then had never reached her ear ;
And when the minstrel won her heart's first token—
A trembling kiss, a raptured vow and tear—
He ever after came, with faith unbroken,
And sang her the sweet songs she loved to hear ;
And told her tales of proud Lord Harold's splendor,
From whom she prayed all angels to defend her.

And, sometimes, when he caught her softly bending
To press the slumbering Bertha's withered cheek,
He felt his soul with all her being blending ;
And when his glowing tongue found words to speak,
He'd bless her for such gentle, tearful tending
On those chained footsteps, now become so weak,
And tell her that Lord Harold loved sincerely,
A mother, too, such as she loved so dearly.

But, when at last he found her truth undying—
Though she believed that he was poor in store—
One morn he came with blazoned banners flying,
And stood, confessed, Lord Harold, at her door ;
And on her pure and generous soul relying,
He clasped her to his noble breast once more,
And bore her off a bride to those proud towers
That rose among a wilderness of bowers.

EDGAR A. POE.

THE ghoul sits by his plundered grave,
  And gnaws his bleeding heart and skull !
While scarce a hand is stretched to save
  All that was once so beautiful.

His lone remains are dragged about
  Through vulgar mire, and scorned and scoffed ;
The fire-work of his life gone out,
  The blackened torch is held aloft.

What though his wondrous soul was thronged
  With pulses choked with fire and flame ?
Such regal madness scarce belonged
  To any other human name.

In whom had such extremes e'er met ?
  To whom such light and darkness given ?
Though hell had his lost feet beset,
  His head blazed in the light of heaven.

THE FIRST BATH.*

ONCE more God leans against the purple bars
That close the rosy portals of the day,
Till, slowly through a mist of fading stars,
Before His shining shoulder they give way,
And outward rolls his treasurer, the sun,
Unpacking gold upon the mountain's height,
And binding trembling glories into one,
Till all the pure, young earth is filled with light;
While wonderous, changing webs of jeweled gauze
From out his great, round coffers of the sea,
Far up the heavens with lustrous hand he draws
To turban up his eastern majesty.

And now they drape him through the sultry hours,
Lest all his splendors, in their noontide glow,
Should fall too fiercely on the new-made flowers
That bless him with their dewy thanks below,
Where work the hidden harvest's golden moles
In tender shoots and still unconscious buds ;
Until, at last, the secret treasure rolls
Through amber vales, or gleams in mellow woods.

* See (*d*) Appendix for Dr. Oliver Wendell Holmes' letter on this poem.

But see!—beneath his warm, declining beam,
One comes, in beauty flashing with surprise,
Superbly naked, to a crystal stream,
The first that ever met her radiant eyes;
And as, with lips apart and quickened blood,
She sudden pauses in the bright retreat,
She sees an angel in the silvery flood
With emerald sandals on her pearly feet.

A moment, and amid the mirrored skies
That seem commingled with the starry sands,
She steals, and, bending in her whiteness, tries
To catch the water spirit in her hands.
Strange, sparkling plashes meet her eye and ear;
And, now, with fervid innocence she sees
The angel stooping, too, within her sphere,
With diamonds rippling round her snowy knees,
Nearer and nearer still, the trembling pair
Approach, half smiling and all eager-eyed,
Until, at last, their forms of earth and air
Melt into one within the dazzling tide.

GERMAN STUDENT'S SONG.

Wine ! skeleton, wine !—Ho ! come let us quaff,
And I'll toll out a song or a churchyard jest,
Till the boom of your deep, sepulchral laugh
Makes the cobwebs shake in your dusty chest.

For the purple lash of this sunny flood
Flogs the lagging pulse till it snaps its chain,
And the fierce, red hoofs of the maddened blood
Dash in fire through the gorges of the brain.

In the sulks of death for a hundred years
You have sat in that mouldy, oaken chair,
In the awful hush of those hollow sneers,
And the gulf of that blind, appalling stare.

Then fill, till the magic works apace,
And the liquid rainbow's bubbling dyes
Flush the dusky stone of your rayless face,
And light the dead signals of your eyes—

Till the muffled feet of your silent soul
Tread the depths of that gloomy vault once more,
And the tide of mirth, sparkling bright as the bowl,
Rolls again through that bolted cavern door.

Wine! skeleton, wine! Ho! come let us quaff,
Till the revel swells to a fearful shout,
And the din of your wild, unearthly laugh
Knocks in red hot cinders my heart about.

WHY DOST THOU TARRY?*

Among the fragrant blossoms of the South
  That blow the golden orange from their lips,
And where from the sweet jasmin's amber mouth,
  The honey-bee its subtle nectar sips,
While, burning through the halo of his wings
  That murmur round him like an unseen lute,
The humming-bird in sudden glory swings
  From dewy bells, like some enchanted fruit;

And where beneath the cool o'erspreading vine,
  Tangled with light the purple shadows sleep,
And emerald waters tremulously shine,
  Or down the dell in jewelled laughter leap,
While through the damasked gloom, on every blast,
  A thousands censers all their perfumes pour;
And Echo, like some memory of the past,
  Sings the sweet songs that wake her, o'er and o'er.

* See Appendix (*b*) for Dr. Holmes' letter on these verse

Why dost thou tarry, maiden of the Spring?
  Think'st thou that there are Northern lips and eyes
That can supply the roses thou would'st bring,
  And compensate us for thy absent skies?
Or think'st thou there are silvery voices here
  That speak the music of those fairy vales,
And balmy sighs whose treasures are as dear
  As the pure incense of thy softest gales?

Come! shining loiterer, come! nor longer stay,
  And let thy leafy gems and opening flowers
Be spilled, like stars along the milky-way,
  Upon this cold, reluctant sod of ours.
Come with thy zephyrs and thy sparkling streams,
  And feathered throng of every throat and plume;
Come with thy coronal of buds and beams——
  Come, fragrant-footed angel of the bloom.

LINES.

ON VIEWING AN EXQUISITELY PAINTED PORTRAIT OF THE BEAUTIFUL
MRS. ROBERT BELFORD.

THIS is no glowing fiction of the brain:
This form and face no fabled charms express,
But here are mirrored simply to explain
A real creation's perfect loveliness.

Yet, we but catch her outward graces here ;
The pencil's skill could not combine with these
Her guileless heart and sympathetic tear,
Her unbought friendships and true charities——

Her silvery laugh—the music of her soul—
Her glorious eyes that hold us in such thrall——
Her regal mein and sweetness whose control
Has made such willing subjects of us all :

But since with these art cannot truly deal——
So much is hidden deep within her breast——
Let us accept all that it may reveal,
For heaven will, one day, blazon all the rest.

CHRISTMAS CHIMES.

I.

Once again !—to the days of the Barons of old,
  When the flagons of silver blazed bright on the board,
          And the bacchanal roared
Amid bucklers and banners and baldricks of gold,
  And the flash of the eye and the flash of the sword ;

When the spears shook aloft their red fingers of steel,
  And the hollow mail clattered and cheered on the
      walls,
          Through the echoing halls,
While the minstrels broke out, and so maddened the
      peal
  That the broad-chested steeds neighed afar in their
      stalls ;

And the revel at last rang so furiously out
  That the arrows, close packed, almost sung in their
      sheaves.

* See (*f*) Appendix for Dr. Holmes' remarks on this poem.

Among helmets and greaves,
And the crossbows and gauntlets that, scattered about,
  Strewed the dark, oaken floor of the castle like leaves ;

When the Lord of the Wassail rose, flushed to the
    brow,
  And, swinging his massive cup high in the air,
      In the torches' red glare,
Pledged the Land of the Holly and Mistletoe-bough,
  Quaffing deep to the brave—deeper still, to the fair ;

While adown to the sea turret, tower, and spire
  In a full-throated chime poured each deep, iron lung,
      And the yule-log's red tongue
Licked the huge stony chops of its cavern of fire,
  As the flame through its murky throat thundered and
    sung ;

And the haughty retainers stood up in a line,
  Before great, smoking haunches, and lustily cheered
      When the boar's head appeared,
And arose from the feast with their beards drenched
    with wine,
  Till the revelry died away, weary and weird.

II.

And once more!   But we turn from the grim days of
    yore
    To the land of the Forest—the Land of the Mine
        That's for thee and for thine—
The Land of the River, the Cedar, the Pine—
    Of the blue, spreading seas, and the cataract's roar,

Where rough wedges of gold pave the broad, husky
    fields,
    And the maple-tree opes its sweet, pelican veins,
        Till its honied store rains,
And the bright, winnowed wealth that the heavy sheaf
    yields
    Lies, like heaps of seed-pearl scattered over the
    plains—

The land where abundance shall never decrease—
    The land of brown toil and the stout pioneer,
        And the swift-footed deer,
That now, must 'mid offerings of pleasure and peace,
    Lay his head on the white altar-stone of the year.

And what though there may not be found at our board
   All the glow of the past, with its crimson and gold,
          And its splendors untold—
With its trappings of war, and its vassal and lord,
   When our blood has been nursed through the brave
      days of old?

And what though we've few ivied abbeys, and towers
   Swinging out on the air their glad festival chimes?
          We've old legends and rhymes,
And great memories to hallow this history of ours
   In the knowledge and light of much happier times.

Then come—while the cup circles joyously now—
   A bright mistletoe-branch of the cedar and pine
          Let us fondly entwine,
And lead some young beauty beneath the green bough,
   And preserve of the past all that's truly divine.

THE GREAT IRON CYCLOPS.

The Great Iron Cyclops came down, through the night,
  At a pace that seemed never to tire ;
And the echoes around him cried out, in affright,
  As he thundered along, in his terrible might,
With his plume of smoke spangled with fire.

And to rival the strides of the tempest he sought,
  'Till it rode, like a footman, behind ;
For his swift, flashing limbs were mysteriously wrought
  Of the brawn and the sinews of ages of thought,
'Till they coped with the speed of the wind.

Through deep-cloven mountains, and valleys he flew,
  And through sullen wastes rugged and bare,
While the cities in handfuls behind him he threw,
  And his breath in hot gusts through his nostrils he
    blew.
As a whale blows the sea in the air.

But through regions of silence and coldness and gloom
  Though he sped his miraculous way,
They burst forth anon into sunshine and bloom,
  While the Spirit of Commerce leaped forth from their
    womb,
And shook out her young plumes to the day ;

For the nations that long had lain buried in sleep,
  Now awoke, with a start, at his roar ;
While the lone maiden ships that had toiled on the
    deep,
  And had pined for a spouse, felt their white bosoms
    leap
As he called them in crowds to the shore.

And still onward he sweeps towards far distant strands
  With his banner of progress unfurl'd,
Binding blue seas together, and linking strange lands,
  And urging the whole human race to strike hands,
'Till one pulse shall pervade all the world !

A ROYAL RACE.

AMONG the fine old kings that reign
  Upon a simple wooden throne,
There's one with but a small domain,
  Yet, mark you, it is all his own.

And though upon his rustic towers
  No ancient standard waves its wing,
Thick, leafy banners flushed with flowers,
  From all the fragrant casements swing.

And here, in royal homespun, bow
  His nut-brown court, at night and morn,—
The bronzed Field-Marshal of the Plough,
  The Chancellor of Wheat and Corn,

The Keeper of the Golden Stacks,
  The Mistress of the Milking-Pail,
The bold Knights of the Ringing Axe,
  The Heralds of the Sounding Flail,

The Ladies of the New-Mown Hay,
   The Master of the Spade and·Hoe,
The Minstrels of the Glorious Lay
   That all the Sons of Freedom know.

And thus, while on the seasons roll,
   He wins from the inspiring sod
The brawny arm and noble soul
   That serve his country and his God

THE PEARL.

THE seasons are but Nature's jewelled ring,
Where, set in changing splendors, we behold
The pearly winter and the em'rald spring,
The ruby summer and the autumn's gold
In the rich ceinture ever varying ;
And where the dazzling fingers of the sun,
That fling the tinted shuttles of the light,
Present the jewels to us one by one,
Forever circling and forever bright,
And where, when all the fervid heats are done,
The cool, pale pearl is turned upon our sight,
That we may revel in a new delight,
And to our Autumn, Spring, and Summer lays
Add yet one other song of grateful praise.

THE MANIAC'S INVOCATION.

THE MANIAC'S INVOCATION.

Stand forth thou gaunt destroyer of our race !
   Know that thou hast no terrors now for me ;
I'd beard thee tyrant to thy very face,
   And spit upon thy rayless majesty.
Uncoil thy hungry worms !—ho ! let them free,
   To banquet on the ruins of this heart ;
I fling the dark repast to them and thee.
   Stand forth, I say again, whate'er thou art !

Ha ! coward, thou would'st steal upon thy prey,
   As that poor, silent sleeper there might tell,
Whose cheek was flushed by thee from day to day
   With the damned vermil of thy surest spell ;
But I, curs't idiot, should have known full well
   Thou wert but fanning her life's coal away
'Till it should blacken in thy nether hell.
   Stand forth, what e'er thou art ! again I say.

THE MANIAC'S INVOCATION.

Through many a long, long night of agony
  With that false meteor thou hast let me grope
By the drear waters of thy starless sea,
  Twisting my very heart strings into rope
To lash her to the last frail plank of hope
  That the cold tide was stealing from her then.
Oh ! I am mighty !—Dar'st thou with me cope ?
  Stand forth, whate'er thou art, I say again.

'Tis madness !—but the fearful frenzy's past,
  Nor shall I name thee, fiend or tyrant now ;
No !—thou wert gentle with her to the last,
  And set thy fairest signet on her brow ;
Then let me to thy sovereign mandate bow :
  But, how can I look on thee as before ?
Thou who hast blasted every pulse !—Yes, thou !
  Stand forth whate'er thou art I say once more !

"ONLY A WOMAN'S HAIR."

Some time after the death of Dean Swift, there was found among his private papers, a small and carefully folded package, bearing the above inscription.

Lone, wayward one who o'er that dark tress lingers
With that strange smile of white-lipped agony
That's but the smothered cry of thy despair,
Where are her darker eyes and rosy fingers,
Or is that all that now is left to thee—
That shining tress " only a woman's hair ? "
Lone, wayward one that aimless o'er it lingers,
Where are her lips and eyes and rosy fingers ?

Has memory fixed thee thus in stone before her
With all thy pulses motionless and mute-
A dumb, deaf statue, blindly kneeling there ;
She the adored, and thou the fierce adorer
Grasping the lute-strings of a broken lute—
That raven lock, " only a woman's hair ? "
Has memory fixed thee thus in stone before her,
She the adored, and thou the fierce adorer?

Oh ! what dread desolation, lost and lonely,
Beneath that ghastly gleam of mirth is hid,
But none shall lay the anguished secret bare,
That's summed and syllabled in that word, " only "
That hollow thud upon the coffin lid.
A woman's hair—" only a woman's hair "—
Oh ! what deep desolation lost and lonely
Is summed and syllabled in that word, " only."

No sign of life—no coming sign or token
To close the door of that dark sepulchre,
But still, that vacant smile and empty stare.
Ah ! surely, surely thy young heart was broken,
And madness came when that was left by her.
That fatal tress—" only a woman's hair,"
No sign of life, no coming sign or token ;
Ah ! surely then, thy poor, young heart was broken.

I'd breathe into thine ear and disenchant thee,
Nor Stella nor Vanessa should I name—
The shadow only of thy love was there—
If I could feign her voice that comes to haunt thee.
I'd breathe *thy* name and turn thee into flame,
While murmuring thus, " only a woman's hair."
I'd whisper in thine ear and disenchant thee,
If I could feign that voice that comes to haunt thee.

TO THE RIGHT-HAND.

I.

Thou great Interpreter of Human Thought,
And Builder in the realms of Wealth and Fame,
Had Archimedes' self that lever brought
To bear upon this globe's gigantic frame,*
Its form and thine had surely been the same :
For thou hast called a mighty world from nought—
The world of Art where all thy works proclaim
That Matter, of whatever grade or kind,
Is simply but the potter's clay of Mind.

II.

Antiquity itself with thee began,
Thou wert the first to draw the jealous line
That runs between the Anthropoid and Man
And makes the latter palpably divine——

* Archimedes is alleged to have said, that if he had an adequate
spot upon which to place a fulcrum, he could construct a lever that
would move the world.

Makes him the climax and the three-fold sign
Of that familiar though unfathomed plan
Where Soul and Spirit their vast strength combine,
Yet, bound as giants by a single mesh,
Lie tangled in the spider's web of flesh.

III.

In vain the mystic problem we essay,
A vail eternal hangs before its face ;
There does not seem to fall one single ray
Upon the age or birth-place of our race.
Whatever foot-prints we attempt to trace
Soon in the gathering darkness fade away,
And we, anon, perceive, with weary pace,
Antiquity itself fall back aghast
Before the deepening gloom of its own past.

IV.

Full-blown beginnings scarce exist in name
Save where the mind refuses to be free ;
The errors of primeval thought became
The matrix of all true philosophy ;
And there are none to solve the mystery—
Not one to question—none to praise or blame,

All—all is lost in dread obscurity—
Is lost because the wherefore and the whence
Transcend the narrow bounds of time and sense.

V.

To solve the origin of things, would be
To fancy some Rosetta-stone of space
That ante-dated its own pedigree
And made the facts ere they had taken place,
So that the Future should the Past embrace ;
Reversing the whole course of destiny
And building from the summit towards the base,
Or, what the crudest intellect rejects,
Placing all causes after their effects.

VI.

Of this stupendous secret we but know
That a dark ocean boundless and sublime,
A Past and Present for its ebb and flow
Once broke in sunlight on the shores of Time.
The depths we fathom or the heights we climb
No further features of the secret show,
Till one might fancy, nor be charged with crime—
But for the signet that all things impress—
That matter was a freak of nothingness

VII.

We need not ask thee what thy Faith of Old.
Or try to catch its ever-varying phase,
Thou didst the gods of early India mould,
And those of Egypt though in later days ;
And altars to Jehovah thou didst raise,
And to his Mightiness the Golden Calf
That's still set up in our most sacred ways,
Where His persuasive influence we feel,
Although the fact we struggle to conceal.

VIII.

But of thy eccentricities of yore,
Thy whims in dates most singular appear.
Right Hand, the pages of our gravest lore
Set forth thy many derelictions here.
How strange that we should doubt and yet revere-
Doubt, that but just three thousand years before,
Man first appeared upon this earthly sphere,
And that with all the time that since has run
We've had but just six thousand years of sun.

IX.

Still, were it not for errors and their ruth,
This world had been a heritage of fools.
Errors are simply but the husks of Truth,
The stripping off of which is but, in sooth,
The methods of all progress and the schools
Where age becomes the antidote of youth,
And, in its wide and deep experience, rules
That Good and Evil, in their seeming strife,
Are simply but the stepping-stones through life.

X.

Only a Myth can serve those higher needs
Where Facts would but discomfiture entail.
There's something in the errors of the Creeds
That each time lifts us higher up to fail ;
And though we never may the Light unvail,
The denser darkness of the gloom recedes
As each succeeding height we slowly scale,
Until at last below us calmly lies
A faint reflection of the upper skies.

XI.

All true philosophy is at its ease,
Because it ever to its lenses brings
A keen, discriminating eye that sees
Infinite greatness in the smallest things,
And can resolve among those hidden strings
All discords into perfect harmonies ;
Suspecting, as it reaches deeper springs,
When all the mazes of the Creeds are trod,
That Devil is but a naughty name for God.

XII.

Those in rapport with Nature's subtle art
Perceive, through their illuminated soul,
That what may seem a blemish in a part
May be a perfect glory of the whole.
Our narrow dogmas shut out the true goal,
And make close corporations of our heart,
Where selfish sentiments alone control.
Although we but receive in what we give,
And, more, in others do but truly live.

XIII.

No casuist has ever yet explained
The sharp conflicting phases of thy will,
For thou through all the ages hast remained
A mighty factor in both good and ill,
Materializing Mind with wondrous skill ;
Lustrous with Virtue and with License stained,
A double destiny thou do'st fulfil,
One half of which is, to the full extent,
The other half's mysterious complement.

XIV.

'Tis curious that thou wert not more alert
In combatting that wily influence
Which did our early history so pervert
With monstrous fancies and absurd pretence,
And foul injustice and false eloquence ;
But then in much of what thou did st assert
We scarce can hold thee guilty of offense,
For touching ancient faiths we know, at least,
That every fact was moulded by a priest.

XV.

Much that is found on hoary brick or stone
May facts and eras truly indicate ;
But, no such tablets ever yet have shown
A single facet, word or line or date
From which our genesis we could collate ;
Nor have those parchments or papyri thrown
The feeblest ray on our benighted state.
But, then, whatever truths in stone or bricks,
A manuscript is very full of tricks.

XVI.

Yet thou hast had such various work to do,
Wert thou consistent it had not been done ;
There was no Old to formulate the New,
In riot Inspiration had begun ;
But there were no true trophies to be won
Till Science and Induction gave the clew,
As seen by some strange webs that had been spun
Where startling mental colors were combined
By artists who, themselves, were color-blind,

XVII.

And here thou wert not favored by the Fates
When thou didst soar on fancy's rainbow wings
To blazon on Creation's morning gates
The wildest of thy wild imaginings
Touching the birth of all terrestrial things,
Which our maturer manhood so berates,
But still to which our childhood fondly clings,
And which, for upwards of three thousand years,
Has set us, shallow doctors, by the ears

XVIII.

How grand, withal, the changes thou has wrought,
And how the world has clothed itself of late,
But strange that all thy battles should be fought
Against the very gods thou did'st create,
And all were in a dazed amorphous state
Had not some bold observant spirit caught
That Fate was Law and Order, not mere Fate,
And that one single link does not contain
The length or involutions of the chain.

XIX.

But time has sapped old legends to the core,
And put our cramped chronology to flight ;
For it can now be proven o'er and o'er,
That ere our queer cosmogony saw light
Or the dim ages of the Troglodyte,
Men, like to those who had long gone before,
Left proof of their existence and their plight
On many a mammoth tusk and reindeer horn—
Aye ! long ere our antiquity was born.

XX.

And what can now be said when now we know
That in the gloomy caves of Cambria *
More than two hundred thousand years ago,
Pre-glacial man had his mysterious day,
And came, like us, to live and pass away ?
Two hundred thousand years ! How dire a blow !
Can Superstition longer stand at bay ?
How worthless here the labors of thy pen,
Where were thy Parchments and Papyri then ?

* See account of discoveries made not long since in the Valley of
Clwyd, North Wales.

XXI.

Here all is mystery ! all is dark and dread.
Save to the brave Iconoclast who feels
That broken idols and beliefs long dead,
Should always pave the temple where he kneels,
But that each outward form of Faith conceals
One shrine at which the hungry soul is fed,
And meets a full response to its appeals—
One altar from all other shrines apart
Set up by Heaven in every human heart,

XXII.

Yet, let me clasp thee and right heartily ;
For though thou first did'st move with sword and flame,
The chisel, brush and pen were all of thee,
And in a broader, nobler chivalry
Thy truest civilizers soon became.
But what endears thee more than all to me
Is that thou did'st affix our struggling name
To that grand Charter that set free the Slave,
And to the world its coming Freedom gave.

TO DR. OLIVER WENDELL HOLMES.

ON HEARING OF THE CELEBRATION OF HIS SEVENTY-SIXTH BIRTH-
DAY.

Though now the splendors of the feast are past
And all the lights are dim, recall the wine !
And let me, though I am the least and last,
Uncovered drain one cup to thee and thine.

Thy pulses I would not awake again ;
But only ask thee—ere mine lose their sway—
To let my more than three score years and ten
Drop this small star into thy Milky-Way.

A JUNE IDYL.

Like a fragrant-footed fawn
Tripping through the silver surf,
Flashing in the azure dawn
On the radiant, rolling turf,

Tost and tinted in the gale
That in sport around her flies,
See her coming through the vale,
Gathering sunlight for her eyes.

Drinking through her sea-shell ears,
Music for her panting throat,
Pouring from the purple spheres
Where the early warblers float ;

Dashing from the opening flowers,
That along her pathway drip,
Clouds of balm and sparkling showers
For the ruby of her lip ;

And inhaling from the thorn,
Odors wafted round her there;
'Till she seems another morn,
She's so balmy, fresh, and fair.

Like a fragrant-footed fawn
Tripping through the silver surf
See her in the rosy dawn
On the radiant, rolling turf.

YES, YES, YOU ARE "A KING."

[Written and inscribed to Henry Wadsworth Longfellow, on reading his poem, "From My Arm-chair," addressed to the children of Cambridge, who had, on his seventy-second birthday presented him a chair made from the wood of the "Village Blacksmith's Chestnut-Tree," which he had long since, immortalized in song.   The poem opens with the lines:

> "Am I a king, that I should call my own,
> This splendid ebon throne?"

Yes, you're "a king," and yet shall call your own
A more resplendent and enduring throne
Than that on which you make the heavens ring.
Yes, yes, you are "a king;" you *are* "a king!"——

A prophet, priest, and king, that has made bloom,
While tabernacled in that sacred room,
A leafless and a withered branch, once more,
As bloomed the Levite's mystic rod of yore,

And filled its blossoms with the harmonies
Of birds, and summer winds, and golden bees,
And children's crystal voices, and the gleams
That now, alas ! but come to us in dreams.

Though through the moss-grown gateway of my years
I look, with outstretched arms, in silent tears
Toward my youth, the prodigal I mourn,
Dead to my grief, refuses to return ;

But when the sainted past inspires your lay,
And I can hear you calling far away,
A deep enchantment on me falls, and then
I am at play in childhood once again.

Such measures fill these barren wastes of ours
With buds, and beams, and fairest fruits and flowers ,
That yet, once more, the suffering soul may sing—
Bethesda's spray, shook from an angel's wing.

You are "a king!" And if for one more gem
There's place in your o'ercrowded diadem,
Take this that now falls glittering on my breast,
And, though unworthy, place it near the rest.

* See (a) Appendix for Mr. Longfellow's letter of acknowledgment.

SERENADE.

See the moon, bright as noon, silvers over the beautiful
    sea,
Where the waves, purple slaves, are waiting Esmali for
    thee,
Till the gale fills our sail as they murmuring bear us
    along,
While, fond dear, in thine ear lost in rapture, I breath a
    low song.
    Echoes ! Echoes ! are warbling in yonder vale ;
    List ! O, list ! 'tis the song of the nightingale.
    Wake ! O, wake ! for the night is waning fast,
    Haste ! O, haste ! ere it's loveliness is past.

  See the moon, bright as noon, silvers over the beauti-
    ful sea,
  Where the waves, purple slaves, are waiting Esmali
    for thee.

Dearest, then hear my prayer.   Linger no longer there.
Open thy casement bars.   Come forth among the stars.
Fly to my arms my love, pure as the heaven above,
This is the witching time.   Haste ere the midnight
    chime.
  See the moon, bright as noon, silvers over the beauti-
    ful sea.
  Where the waves, purple slaves, are waiting Esmali
    for thee.

IDOLATRY.

Whether we prostrate fall or bend the knee,
Or bow with faces turned towards the east,
Whate'er the creed, or color of the priest,
Are we not guilty of Idolatry?

To us all Nature, eloquent and terse,
Simply presents a great Primeval Cause
Immutable of essence and of laws——
The Guide and Author of the universe.

A mystery uncreate, whose secret springs
Set all created faculties at naught,
That does not come within the range of Thought,
Or scope of the Analysis of things.

A wondrous whole with neither form nor parts,
That we attempt in various shapes to seize,
To satisfy those small philosophies
That so contract and honeycomb the heart.

Whatever semblances we may adore,
They're all in essence palpably the same,
And differ only as to form and name :
They are but myth and matter to the core.

But who shall venture to condemn us here?
Is it not darkness groping for the light—
The finite yearning for the infinite
That never comes though ever drawing near?

Some idol seems the souls necessity ;
It is a declaration of our need
Of something more than mortal for our creed—
A something that we fain would feel and see.

Thus, one conception centering in the whole,
Unites all faiths, both rude and civilized—
By all one unseen power is recognized,
That holds the universe in its control.

So that despite the daintiness we feel
In touching skirts with others in the street,
At whatsoever shrine we chance to meet,
There's one broad plank on which we all can kneel.

Though gods should crowd our sanctuary shelves,
Our heart of hearts may still be pure and free,
There's only danger in idolatry
When we set up the idol of ourselves.

THE VICTOR.

In the full flush of her sweet maidenhood,
  A fair young peasant, weary of the way,
Sat down to rest within a summer wood,
  But soon among the wild flowers sleeping lay.

A youth, of high degree and ardent soul,
  By chance came dreaming through the dim retreat;
And all unconsciously upon her stole,
  'Till, startled, he beheld her at his feet.

So helpless she and of such lowly mien,
  It seemed as though none cared for the sweet maid;
But, had he other eyes, he might have seen
  Two angels standing near her in the shade.

He gazed enchanted on her lovely face,
  Now turned, in some sweet dream, toward the skies,
When, struck with all her innocence and grace,
  He, too, looked upward with imploring eyes.

And silently his red lips moved in prayer
   When suddenly a change came o'er his brow ;
And he no longer stood bewildered there
   For sweet compassion filled his bosom now

He asked for what had freely been bestowed,
   Strength to be noble, generous and true ;
And, while his heart with gratitude o'erflowed,
   One of the angels closer to him drew

When stooping gently forward, where he stood,
   He placed a rosebud on the sleeper's breast ;
And then stole noiselessly from out the wood,
   And left her to her purity and rest.

But when she woke, and, wondering, found the flower,
   There stood but one bright angel by her side ;
The other had gone forth, and, from that hour,
   Became, through life, the youthful Victor's guide

THE WAIF.

Oh ! poor little barefooted, hollow-cheeked thing,
How early dost thou and thy destiny meet ;
Neither bright bud nor blossom thou comest in spring,
But a windfall of childhood struck down at our feet.

How aged and how cold the sad light of those eyes,
And how quenched every tint on that sorrowful face.
Where we find as we seek for thy lips' rosy dyes
But the trembling blue lines of dead joy in their place.

Lonely waif, tossed about mid the winds and the rain,
In this terrible struggle for shelter and bread,
Oh, 'tis well that thou hast but one feeling of pain—
That of hunger and cold ;—all the others are dead !

Then, come to my arms, meanly clad as thou art,
Till the anguish that wastes thee, for once is beguiled ;
Lay thy head on my breast, with thine ear to my heart,
Till it rocks thee to sleep, my poor, barefooted child.

TO ————.

Once more! once more! enchantress, or I die.
Break not the spell that chains my ravished ear,
But let me in those wondrous transports lie,
As tremblingly my pulses pause to hear
That soft low gush that, blending with thy lyre,
Calls up thy spirit to that dark blue eye
That's floating in a wave of liquid fire.

But stay!—such beauty cannot be its own
Without the dazzling wing and golden hair;
Then tempt not heaven, that sees thee thus alone,
To break the lovely chrysalis that's there,
And fix my upward-gazing destiny,
Till all my being settles into stone,
And leaves me but a monument to thee.

Then, where a trace of thee?—The sculptor's art,
Or pencil dipt in fancy's purest springs,
Or dreaming poet's wild imaginings
Wrought to the full intensity of bliss,
Would all, with their vain Icarian wings,
Fall coldly back upon my widowed heart.—
No language for that blinding, burning kiss!
No touch that swelling bosom can impart!

THE APRIL SHOWER.

Come, chase me!—chase me, April shower!
That I once more may run away;
For, oh! 'tis many a weary hour
Since you and I were last at play—
Since last my heart lay in my eyes,
And sunshine lived upon my face—
Since last I watched the April skies,
And dipped my head to take a race.

'Twas evening—I remember well—
An eve of joy and balm and love,
When merry hearts met in a dell—
A spot scooped out within a grove—
And there, while on a primrose-raid,
Not sparing the unopened bud,
A bright one clapped her hands and said,
"An April shower comes through the wood!"

THE APRIL SHOWER.

Though ofttimes we had met at school,
I had not seen her till that hour !
So I stood playing "April fool,"
While she stood crying, " April shower ! "
Till down, at last, the silvery flood
Came glittering in the setting sun,
And caught us brightly where we stood,
Just as we were about to run.

So being deserted by the rest,
Who laughing thought to beat the cloud,
I simply drew her to my breast
And o'er her head in shelter bowed ;
But soon a strange affair took place,
Beyond all explanation's power ;
When she upturned her shaded face,
'Twas radiant with an April shower !

GOD HELP HER.

God help the wretch who nightly drags
Her life along the ghastly flags,
In sin, in hunger, and in rags.

God help her, when the bitter rain
Beats on her—like a window pane—
And almost washes out her stain.

God help her, when, with bleeding feet,
She pauses ere she stoops to meet
The cruel corner of the street.

God help her, when, with tearless eye,
She looks into the blackened sky,
And strikes her breast and asks to die.

GOD HELP HER.

God help her, wandering to and fro
Without one pitying look to throw
A gleam upon her sullied snow.

Poor child of good, and child of ill,
The slave of her misguided will,
God help her!—she's a woman still.

TO THE NEW MOON.

Ah, moon !—ah, cunning moon, thou art not young ;
For, upwards of three thousand years ago,
The silent music of thy silvery tongue
Was trembling in Arcadian vales, we know.

And though thou seem'st so bright and youthful still,
Thou, in the fostering fullness of thy charms,
Didst stretch thy white limbs on the Cælian Hill,
And clasp young Tuscan Roma in thine arms.

And, e'en through grim, old Thebes, in majesty
Thou didst thy midnight glories proudly trail ;
When the cold Memnon should have sung to thee
And kept for sunrise his funereal wail.

Strange ! that the dull colossus was not won
By the soft pressure of those beamy hands
That never smote him as oft did the sun,
When bursting from its sleep of burning sands.

But, wert thou not in Eden, fresh and fair,
When Eve first slept upon its dewy sward?
And didst thou not weave diamonds in her hair,
And revel in her eyes, as thy reward?

Ah, moon !—ah, cunning moon, thou art not young,
Though clear, in these bright skies, thy tranquil brow,
Heaven's censer of pure light thou there hast hung
From age to age, as thou art hanging now.

WINTER.

When Winter, that crusty old rogue, brushing by,
    Plucks our woods just as if they were geese,
Oft I notice a smile in his merry, gray eye,
As he sends their brown tatters adrift through the sky
    To play shadows among its white fleece.

'Tis because that his lot is not hard after all,
    For, while travelling onward, he knows,
When he shakes a sweet shrub or a forest tree tall,
That the seeds of wild roses, and acorns fall
    In the print of his frosty old toes.

And this hint with a lesson I'm sure should be rife
    To those wretched old croakers of ours,
Whose teeth and short nails are forever at strife,
And who never can see that the blasts throughout life
    Always scatter the seeds of some flowers.

THE HUSBANDMAN.

Hail ! sunburnt glory of the plough—
The noblest work that heaven has made—
With clustering gems upon thy brow,
While wielding thus that sceptre-spade,
That swarthy hand in mine be laid ;
For I would grasp it bravely now,
And see thee stride across the plain
Scatt'ring these showers of amber grain
That fall like gusts of golden rain
Along the mellow, furrowed sod
That lies, the open Hand of God.

Behold the heritage that's thine.
With fretted dome and crystal walls !
Behold the palace lamps that shine—
Sun, moon and stars—throughout its halls ;
Behold its fountain-waterfalls,
Its fleecy flocks and gentle kine ;
And on its landscape-gardens look,
Where nestles many a shady nook
Beside its sweet-toned silver brook ;
And wouldst thou, then—a worthless thing—
Droop in the hovel of a King ?

THE ANGELS OF THE BLIND.*

Though on the dark, drear walls of the lonely blind
    man's skull
  A picture is never hung by the glowing hand of light,
But in the gloomy catacomb his brain beats thick and
    dull,
  Like some huge, lazy death-watch slowly wearing
    out the night ;

And though along the pavement of that cavern never
    pours
  One beam of all the beauty or the life that 'round us
    teems,
And Nature, as in wantonness, has shut its outer doors,
  And almost made a desert of the very land of dreams ;

---

  * Voices, alone, are the visitants of the dreams of those born blind.
Just as in their waking state, all besides is dark and void.

Yet, there are viewless angels that surround him night
  and day,
    Who sport throughout that sepulchre as if it were a
      grove,
And though he never sees them, still he hears their
      wings at play,
    And knows they are the voices of the ones he learned
      to love.

ONE HOPE.

ONE HOPE.

Oh! God, the floodgates of this heart of mine,
So long shut down, in madness, against Thee,
Have burst, at last, before another shrine,
Beneath a deluge of idolatry
That sweeps, with all its desolating powers,
The few full chords Thy name alone inspires,
As Ætna sweeps some fated spot, where flow'rs
Might long have bloomed but for its headlong fires.

And, yet, before no pagan gold I kneel,
As knelt the faithless Israelites of old;
I have not felt, nor can I ever feel
One pulse for aught that's passionless or cold;
For never has a fibre of this brain,
Throbbed to tame grief or pleasure's fancied spell;
But strung to agonizing bliss or pain,
Owns but the heaven of one, or th' other's hell.

Then, teach me how to supplicate Thine Ear,
That Thou would'st break the bonds that shut me in ;
I'd weep, but then I'd shed too bright a tear,
There's so much rapture mingled with my sin ;
Yet, teach me not !--One hope has not yet flown—
The hope that when in anger Thou'rt arrayed,
Thou wilt remember that by Thee, alone,
The breathing idol of my soul was made.

A FATHER TO HIS SLEEPING CHILD.

How like thy mother—every circling hour
As thus I gaze, more fully I can trace
The beauteous semblance of that faded flow'r
          In thy sweet face.

Dear miniature of her who's sainted now,
Her wonted smile seems sweetly lingering there :
And that dark tress which shades thy shining brow,
          Is her own hair.

Oh, let this fervent kiss thy slumbers mar,
That I may gaze upon her speaking eye,
Which seem'd a fragment of the vesper star
          And deep blue sky.

Sleep on, sleep on, thou lonely lovely thing ;
Owe the unruffled calmness of thy breast
To thy own angel mother's golden wing
          That guards thy rest.

THE STORM FIEND.

" Ho ! ho ! "—said a sprite, at the dead of the night,
As he rose from the Danube's chill wave,
"The winds moan as wild as a desolate child,
And the world is as drear as the grave.

" Not a glimmering ray lights the traveller's way
As he gropes on the verge of yon steep,
And the sailor's stout bark, through the tempest dark,
Wildly rolls o'er the face of the deep.

"See that monk with gray hairs, telling o er his prayers,
While the storm swings the old Convent bell,
He is seized with strange fears, as he fancies he hears
A low knock at the door of his cell.

"And that beautiful girl, all rose, jet and pearl,
Who starts from her slumbers, so pale,
How she qualls like a fawn as she peeps for the dawn
Thro' the casement that flaps in the gale.

" Ha ! ha !" said the sprite, and he chuckled outright,
As the winds swept more rapidly past,
" 'Tis the rarest of glee for a rider like me
To bestride such a terrible blast.

" With the lightning's red veins for my measureless reins,
And a cloud-saddle fastened beneath,
My chargers shall fly through earth, ocean and sky,
'Till I win me a witherless wreath."

Then on them he swung, while the rocky hills rung,
As they trampled and fumed in their pride,
And the thunder's loud thwack, as it fell on their back,
Seemed to tell forth each measureless stride.

So onward they dash'd, they so madly were lashed,
With the speed that the meteor moves,
While his demon-like mirth grew more fierce as the
        earth
Staggered under their hurricane hoofs.

But morning it came with its flushes of flame,
And the tempest deprived of its powers,
Sobbed itself into calm amid sunshine and balm,
And at last fell asleep 'mong the flowers.

But it came in too late, for the traveller's fate
Was then sealed by a hand cold and stiff;
With a cry long and wild for his wife and his child,
He was swept off that shuddering cliff.

And the mariner's sail, left a wreck by the gale,
Was now crashing 'mid ocean's dark caves,
While the sailors in crowds hanging dead in the shrouds,
Turned green in the light of the waves.

And the monastery fell, for its turret and bell
Stood aloft in the whirlwind's pass,
And the quivering trunk of the gray-headed monk
Was dug out from beneath the huge mass.

But the saddest of all was the gentle one's fall
Who look'd out from her casement aghast.
The warm dew of repose that hung on the sweet rose,
It was chill'd by the winds as they passed.

And she droop'd from that hour, the poor delicate flow'r,
Tho' a youth pray'd and wept by her side;
But his tears were in vain, though they fell fast as rain,
For ere long on his bosom she died.

Then so wild his despair, when her dark glossy hair
Fell in clouds on her bosom of snow,
That he rush'd from the crowd, with a laugh long and
     loud,
In the last fearful refuge of woe.

And now on yon peak, rugged, dizzy and bleak,
That but whispers back ocean's dull roar,
In the depths of despair he oft battles the air,
A poor maniac, lost evermore.

And when in their might the winds traverse the night,
And the face of the sky is o'ercast,
He laughs at the screams of the seagull, and dreams
That he stabs the curst fiend of the blast.

OLIVER WENDELL HOLMES.

In this lone wilderness of rhyme,
  Surrounded by a thirsty flock,
He lifts his rod, with hand sublime,
          And smites the rock,

'Till where the voiceless desert lay,
  Throughout a waste of cheerless hours,
A living fount begins to play
          On sudden flowers.

And as his way he onward wends,
  With all the Hebrew's matchless power
He looks towards Heaven, and lo ! descends
          The manna shower.

And having fed the famished crowd,
  'Till more than sated each desire.
He goes before a pillar'd cloud,
          Or disc of Fire !

CREATION.

All heaven is lost in silence !—and the cry
Of cherubim and seraphim is hushed,—
Angel and rapt archangel prostrate lie,
Beneath a weight of sudden glory crushed ;
And conquering hosts, in burning panoply,
Are, like a troubled ocean, backwards pushed !

The Spirit of the Throne is passing by !
And veiled so thinly is his radiant face,
That the resplendent lightnings of his eye
Flash out upon yon cheerless realms of space,
Kindling them up into a morning sky
That clasps infinity in its embrace.

Downwards he sweeps through their young trembling
His footsteps blazing forth in orbs of light—   [dyes—
While the huge dust—that from his sandals flies,
In countless worlds begins its ceaseless flight ;
And darkness, mid the shining conquest, lies
Trodden beneath the power of his might.

And, now, while gazing on the new born day,
A mighty chorus thunders to His name
Who sent the red spheres on their circling way,
And dipt the rayless void in living flame ;
And as the last grand " Glory " fires the lay,
" The morning stars " take up the wonderous theme.

MON BIJOU.

My heart's own brilliant, set in living pearls,
Deep in that cluster of sweet little girls
Who, playfully forestalling time and care,
'Twine threads of silver with thy raven hair;
How oft am I, fond jeweller, afraid
That death will steal upon my stock in trade,
And tear the ondrous treasure from my breast.
Oh! should one sparkling gem be snatched away,
What shatter'd light around that group would play;
How sadden'd all the lustre of the rest,
And how could I unlearn one dear, dear name;
Or, through a weary waste of sunless years,
Gaze on my broken bijou, but through tears;
As vainly I would make it look the same,
And ofttimes close my poor, dim eyes to trace
The outlines of that long-lost, darling face?
But, why this shadow resting on my brow,
When thou art near—when thou hast to me giv'n
Another life that lies almost in heav'n;
When all my jewels glitter round thee now,
As if from solid sunshine they were hewn
At sapphire morn, at ruby eve, or crystal noon?

FRAGMENT.

FRAGMENT.

When, in his strength, the monarch of the air
Soars proudly through the azure fields of heaven,
His pinions burning in the noontide glare,
Or flashing in the deep-red dyes of even,
He sees the earth receding from his eye,
And looking round him, in his chainless glee,
Utters a loud, a long, wild, ringing cry,
And that's the joyous shout of liberty.

But, when he leaves these vast ethereal plains,
And falls into the fowler's hidden snare,
Beneath the icy pressure of his chains,
How soon his sounding wing hangs listless there;—
And oft, as o'er their galling links he broods,
Dreaming of the bright hours when he was free,
He looks up through the shining solitudes,
And shrieks—the bitter shriek of slavery.

If thus 'tis from the eagle to the dove,
Say, how can we upon our fetters smile,
Save those that, woven by the hand of love,
Are 'round us flung with many a tender wile?
So pure a shrine of freedom is the soul,
That could our chains lose all their weight and chill,
And, twined with light, extend from pole to pole
We'd sigh—and feel that we were captives still.

TYRE.

On the spot where now 's scattered the fisherman's
    home,
Stood the rival of Carthage the rival of Rome ;
But, how vainly we seek in its shade, to behold
E'en a trace of the greatness that marked it of old :
Long locked in the merciless grasp of decay,
For ages its ruins have moulder'd away.

'Tis the curse of Omnipotence rests on thee, Tyre !
Eternally plunged in the gulf of his ire,
·One glimmering of hope is forbidden to shine
Through the gloom of that terrible sentence of thine ;
The flame of thy glory extinguished at last,
Thou shalt moulder forever, a wreck of the past !

Say, where is the flash of the Syrian gem
That hung upon Ithobaal's diadem,
When, in purple and gold, all your princes bow'd,
As he pass'd with a shout through the shining crowd ?
'Tis fled with the gleam of the treasures untold,
That built up thy temples and idols, of old.

IMAGE EVALUATION
TEST TARGET (MT-3)

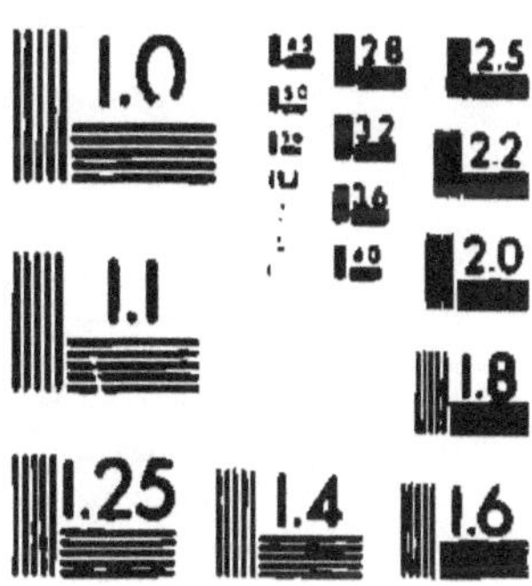

Or, where is the broidered Egyptian sail,
That unbosomed its beautiful hues to the gale,
'Till thy galleys stretch'd out o'er the ocean at even,
Seemed the fringe of the golden tinged drapery of
        heaven
Or the shores of some far away fairy Isle
That glittered and glowed in the sun's last smile?

All are gone! and the voice of thy mirth is no more;
The Sidonian's song, and the Bashan oar,
The chariot, the horseman, the Grecian slave,
The wealth of the mine and the Indian wave,
The Grammadim's strength, the Arvadian's tread,
Are things that have long passed away with the dead!

The God who shakes heaven, and earth beneath,
When his shining brand flies from its thunder cloud
        sheath——
Who rolls up in slumbers the wings of the storm,
And melts into moonlight its terrible form,
Has trodden thee down in the strength of his ire,
Oh!—desolate!—desolate!—desolate Tyre!

LOST.

Spattered like blood on the face of the angry sky,
A red flag, blown into tatters, half mast high,
   Signals a ship far off in the deepening gloom ;
Her strong ribs wrung like withes in the tempest's gripe
That thunders a death-song down through her rocking
     pipe,
   And ploughs into smoke the pathway of her doom.

The battle-door of the waters swoops to the shock,
And strikes her as if she were but a shuttlecock,
   Knocking her almost keel up into the air,
Where, trailing with shattered yards and tangled shrouds,
She looms like a spectre sail among the clouds,
   Till tumbled back with her quivering planks swept
     bare.

Hung with dark cataracts that pour from every spar
And deluge her lofty, livid beacon star,
    Still through the awful tumult she keeps afloat,
And onward rolls while the cold, black ghastly tide
Leaps through huge arteries ruptured in her side,
    And washes the dull death-rattle into her throat.

But thundering now amid sunken reefs and wrecks,
A pale-faced host surges o'er her yawning decks,
    Staring the gloom into strange, blind, deadly light;
Till one long murderous crash and unearthly yell
In dying echoes boom through the watery hell,
    And leave the great, round sea alone with the night.

THE DREAMER.

I've a world of my own! I've a world of my own,
   That is brighter by far, and more happy than this;
A creation so pure that the spirit alone
   Is permitted to taste of its fountains of bliss;
Where the mystical drops, though they glance but in
     dreams,
   May be quaff'd with an exquisite thrill to the last,
For the depths where they sparkle are fed by those streams
   That still sprinkle with verdure the waste of the past.

I've a world of my own! I've a world of my own,
   With its morning—of blushes that waken no more;
With its noontide—of smiles that once brilliantly shone;
   And its starlight—of eyes whose last beamings are o'er.
And thither from earth I oft wing my lone flight,
   To revisit the scenes that to me were so dear,
And to listen again to that phantom of light
   That was once all that heaven could grant to me here.

I've a world of my own! I've a world of my own ;
  A bright spot in this desert-like bosom of mine ;
Where I meet with the spirit of joys that are flown,
  In an oasis blooming 'round memory's shrine.
With the shadows I cherish, there, there let me dwell—
  Would the hand not be cold that could tear us apart?
Gaze in silence and sadness, but break not the spell—
  Wake me not!—wake me not, from—that dream of
    my heart.

GRAND OVERTURE.

[AN EXTRAVAGANZA.]

At the first, red sweep of the Lightning's baton,
.The drums of the Thunder all rolled out,
Till the rocks that the Earth's pale audience sat on,
In the startled gloom, seemed to dance about.

When, the treble Winds, set in mighty motion,
Hurried down, amain, with a deafening roar,
While the ponderous double-bass of the Ocean
Boomed sublimely on through the awful score.

And the alto Hills rang aloud, to falling,
As the swift bolt sang to their inmost cores ;
And the shout of the tenor Woods was appalling,
As they swung and leaped on the shuddering shores.

And the grand accord filled all climes and places,
Until Nature's ribs shook with vast applause,
And a host of cities fell on their faces
In the "bravo!" rift of the Earthquake's jaws.

Till, at last, from a close of dread " pianos,"
The *finale* burst with a crash of rage,
And the skies gave way o'er the red volcanoes
That flamed out in footlights along the stage.

MORN.

With sunbeams her rosy-tipped buskins she ties,
   As downward she steps on the purple-brow'd hills ;
While a flood of stained glory breaks forth from her eyes,
   And runs down to the valleys, like long, shining rills.

O'er the green and gold seas of the landscape below,
   See the lark hangs aloft, like a musical star—
So begemmed are his plumes in the amaranth glow,
   That now gathers apace round the wheels of her car.

And all nature awakens thro' earth and through air,
   In the sweet-scented breeze that's beginning to rove ;
While the fawn, rising up, all bedewed, from her lair,
   Like a mass of brown silver leaps off through the
     grove.

THE SPELL.

Lone, dark and spectral thou art standing there—
A pile of tombstones in the babbling street,
Whose shadows, tangled round my leaden feet,
Are the sure, early grave-clothes that I wear.

In vain I seek to pass in the disguise
Of hurried footsteps and averted brain ;
Thy spell is on me, and I must remain
To look into that window's guilty eyes :—

To look into the chamber where he lay,
And hear, once more, with heavy dropping head,
The agonizing cry, "he's dead ! he's dead !"
And be too strong, again, to faint away :

And linger, in my stupid misery,
To catch the dull, low shuffling on the stairs
When they are coming down in silent pairs
With what would seem God's broken word to me;

When they are bearing to the hungry tomb
The last, dead sunbeam of my darkened years,
That leaves me, e'en without the light of tears
To stagger out my life in deepening gloom.

TENNYSON !

Lord of the thunder-toned, colossal lyre
Whose huge, harmonious cables swing, sublime,
O'er the foundations of thy monument
Those ponderous masses of immortal rhyme—
Vast, glowing blocks of adamantine fire,
That bid defiance to all change and time,
From proud Parnassus by the lightning rent,
Until, at last, its total bulk shall lie
Beneath thy feet, and thou shalt upwards climb
Into the great, broad, startled firmament.
There thou shalt blaze, half hid from mortal eye,
Above the glorious sea of the last cloud,
Where never shadow quarrelled with the sun,
Or tempest raged, unbitted, to and fro.
There, thou shalt mark the pilgrim nations come
To chant thy deep-toned symphonies below,
And, when the booming chorusses are done,
Behold them wave ten thousand hands on high,
Towards thy fierce-flaming head that cleaves the sky,
And shout, "Hail Tennyson !—immortal Tennyson !"

THE PRISONER.

Down by the waters of the Don* to-night.
A poor young prisoner gazes on the stars
Through a deep loop-hole curst with iron bars
Whose ruffian shadows in their rudeness smite
The feeble ray that trembles on his cheek,
As, with a heart too sad and full to speak,
He weeps the loss of innocence and light.

Beside him in his close, dark, dreary cell.
In restless sleep a hoary villain lies,
Foul visions sporting with his glassy eyes
That seem the portals of his inner hell
Flashing and failing in its fitful fires,
With horrible resolve that never tires
Till morning comes to break the fearful spell.

* A sluggish river on which the jail at Toronto, Canada, is built.

All the day long in that pale watcher's ears,
The ribald song, and jest's unholy din
Drowned the low whisperings of his soul within ;
But now, in silence and in bitter tears,
He mourns the crime that he must expiate
In the dark dungeons of a Christian State,
By learning how to sin away his years.

The noxious vapors, from the sedgy lake,
That ooze through that dim opening, damp and chill,
Check the warm current of his heart's red rill ;
And now, till all his miseries awake,
There crowd in memory on his sickening brain,
The breeze, the sunshine, and the blessed rain
That lit up the pale wild flower in the brake.

He watches ;—for ere morn the moon shall trace
Her path across his narrow strip of sky ;
And he would gaze upon her passing by,
To see if any love shone in her face ;
For all the world had left him in distrust,
And he was trodden down into the dust,
A wretched, helpless outcast of his race.

For like the Spartan moralists of old,
The great adroit, who featly play their part,
Hate him for being a sloven in their art ;
While had he been more practiced or more bold,
He might have clad his crimes in purple dyes,
And dazzled out a sordid nation's eyes
With the broad splendor of his cursed gold.

But now, while gasping for more room and air,
A glory, frightened from his dungeon walls,
Upon his pallid brow serenely falls :
It is the moon !—But no ! How strange and fair !
It is his sainted mother's gentle eyes
That bend, till dawn, upon him from the skies,
And turn him into dreaming marble there.

THE HUMMING BIRD.

Purple, golden, burning mote,
As among the flowers you float,
Not a single, silvery note
                Falls on my ear.
Come, starlet tune your dazzling throat ;
                I pause to hear.

How, hung amid a thousand dyes,
A prism, you glitter in my eyes,
To every bud that round you lies
                In emerald set ;
A rainbow that the summer skies
                Ne'er equalled yet.

But, hist ! You are not silent, bird ;
The air with melody is stirred,
As soft as some low, whispered word
                Through breathing strings ;
The song denied your throat is heard
                Among your wings.

And had it thrilled with more delight,
You are so beautiful and bright,
In gazing, all its sweetness might
                Forgotten be;
Its murmuring shadow then is quite
                Enough for me.

BEARLA FEINE. *

Fountained behind that dark mysterious veil
That long has mocked the gaze of prying sages,
Oh ! great word-river of the mighty Gael,
Sublimely rolling down the steep of ages—
Ancient of tongues, that first began to flow,
Ah, who shall dare to say, how long ago ?

Nor stately Latin, nor imperial Greek,
E'en 'though intoned by Virgil and by Homer,
In love or war or peace like thee can speak—
Thou gentle, restless, headlong, world-wide roamer,
The priceless treasures of whose matchless lore
Like golden sands strew almost every shore.

When surging through the patriot's glowing soul,
Tearing the floodgates of his lips asunder
With power that neither knows nor brooks control,
Who'd think the stormy flood that leaps in thunder,
Erewhile had whispered o'er the rose and pearl
That tint the sweet mouth of the Kerry girl ?

* Ancient Fenian Celtic.

When, standing in the empty womb of space,
The Great I Am the silence first had broken,
When light and darkness first met face to face,
What then the sovereign language that was spoken,
The words that ushered in the primal dawn?
Was the sublime command—" Biols lus awn? "

What though ungrateful Saxon knaves and fools
Combine to rob thee of thy ancient glory,
And trace to other founts and later schools
The riches of their language, song and story,
Their " Furthoc " was not yet, nor was their name,
When thou had'st had a thousand years of fame.

But vain the regicidal war has been ;
Thou hast baptized their valleys, hills and mountains :
The royal impress of thy Beith Lus Nuin
Is found among their rocks and streams and fountains.
Thou art alone the key that opes the door
That guards the dungeons of their early lore.

The test and touchstone, thou, of those weak tongues
That 'round their birth build such imposing fables,
Though they had not the strength of brain or lungs
To read aloud the famed Eugubine Tables
That baffled all their empty-headed pride
Till thou did'st lave them in thy kindred tide.

LINES.

How oft, while wandering through some desert place,
I've met a poor, pale, thirsty little flower
Looking towards heaven, with its patient face,
In dying expectation of a shower.

．

And when the sweet compassion of the skies
Fell like a charm upon its sickly bloom,
O, what a grateful stream gushed from its eyes
Towards Him who cared to snatch it from the tomb.

And O, when all its leaves seemed folding up
Into the tender bud of other days,
What clouds of incense, from the deep'ning cup,
Rolled upwards with the burden of its praise.

LINES.

And then I thought, in this fair land of ours
How few who feel affliction's chastening rod,
Are like the poor, pale, thirsty little flowers,
With their meek faces turned towards their God—

How few, when angry clouds and storms depart,
And all the light of heaven reappears,
Are found with incense rising in a heart
Dissolved before His Throne in grateful tears.

AH ! YES—AH, YES !

Ah ! yes—for I remember well,
"Twas in the summer-twilight hour
Within a sweet secluded dell,
Where scarce the sunbeams ever fell,
Although the cowslips felt their power;
And every time there came a shower,
Perfumed it with a fragrant smell,
And shook out all their loveliness,
"Twas long ago—Ah ! yes—Ah, yes !

"Twas close beside a silvery brook
That sang its journey through the vale,
Where willows in a golden stook,
Enclosed her in a lovely nook ;
The while the amorous scented gale
Crept softly through their trembling pale,
And toyed with each dark shining tress,
'Twas there we met—Ah ! yes—Ah, yes !

A chaplet of wild buds and leaves
Were twined about her graceful head,
Such as some midnight fairy weaves,
Or from her tiny queen receives
To lay on some sweet dreamer's bed,
That she, while her fair bosom heaves,
May twine it with a raven tress,
'Twas thus she sat—Ah! yes—Ah, yes!

Her eyes from out the water came,
Soon as my footsteps stirred the grass,
Two wondrous orbs of mellow flame,
With hidden depths that none may name,
And power that would not let me pass,
And I remained, alas! alas!
And trembling there stood to confess
How lost I was—Ah! yes—Ah, yes!

The words we spoke I cannot tell;
But they were hurried, warm and wild,
And as from both our lips they fell,
They round us wrought a deeper spell,
And all our being so beguiled
That e'en the very passing child
The frenzy of our love could guess,
And frenzy 'twas—Ah! yes—Ah, yes!

The dream has long since passed away ;
And I am still beside that stream ;
But oh ! how altered, old and gray,
And oh ! how dim the waters play,
Because, because of that lost beam,
That touched them with a sunny gleam
When she had in her loveliness
Breathed in my ear—Ah ! yes—Ah ! yes.

THE STORM.

Dark billows heave against the angry west,
Where dying daylight struggles in his blood,
With one dim sun-shaft quivering in his breast,
That pins him down upon the gloomy flood.

The sullen winds their mighty wings unfurl,
And hastening clouds a hurried phalanx form,
Till sudden darkness seems at last to hurl
The globe from out the pathway of the storm.

Down! down it comes!—as when the angels fell—
Blacker and swifter still in all its ire,
Striking the ocean into such a hell
As beggars the red majesty of fire.

All nature seems to miss her rocky feet;
Pale cities, fleets and tottering hills give way;
And palsied man creeps from his dark retreat,
To see if all is o'er, or it be day.

THE BELLE.

O, my beautiful child with that exquisite waist
That's as small as a wasp's, it's so charmingly laced,
 How delightful you're looking to-day :
For your brow is as white as the lily that blows,
And your delicate cheeks are just touched with the rose,
And your lips,—Don't be coughing, I pray.

And your eyes are so large and so wond'rously bright,
That they seem, at this moment, strange fountains of
  light
 With their depths so exhaustless and clear ;
And your hands are so tiny, transparent and fair,
That the sun's shining through them, just now, I de-
  clare,
And your breast,—Don't be coughing my dear.

Oh, to-night how enchanting you'll look at the ball,
For such beauty as yours must outrival them all,
 But I see that you're drowsy, poor dove.
Ah, you slumber my darling, such slumber is balm,
For I've never before seen your bosom so calm,
And I'm glad you're not coughing, my love.

'TIS ALL BUT A DREAM AT THE BEST.

IT is all but a dream at the best, so they say,
But what recks it as long as the dreamers are gay,
And believe that they snatch an occasional kiss
From the lips of the beautiful phantom of bliss?
The soul owes some thrills of its purest delight
To the mystical spells of the visions of night,
For it never quaffs deep of the Lethean stream,
"Till it clasps all it ever can love in a dream.

When the spirits of those who enchant us by day,
From the scenes of their exile, at eve steal away
And, unsullied by earth, their bright revelries keep
In the home of the heart—the Elysium of sleep,
"Tis kind heaven that lengthens and lightens their chain,
"Till they visit those magical regions again,
That were lost, with the depths of their treasures un-
    told,
By the beautiful rebel who trod them of old.

But say, were they dreams that so widely o'ercast
The dark cycles entombed in the gulf of the past?
Were the shackles then fastened on millions unborn
Like shadows that melt in the beams of the morn?
And now, can the tear that dims misery's eye,
Can the beggar boy's prayer, and the dungeon's deep
   sigh,
Can the wrongs of a nation, the shrieks of a slave
Be mere traces in sand on the verge of a wave?

But should science now yoke to her glittering car
All the demons of discord, the terrors of war,
And with laurels besmeared with the blood of mankind,
Mount the angel of death on the wings of the wind,
Till the cities of earth fall a prey to the flame
That before had encircled with glory their name;
Oh! how dreadful her triumph!—how gory its beam!
If a dream, would not this be a terrible dream?

THE REQUIEM.

Yawning a sudden gulf of stormy gloom,
Day, dying, dropt his under jaw in night
And headlong fell into an ebon tomb
That quenched his broken diadem of light.

Yet through the matted darkness of his shroud,
His blood-shot eye a moment wildly stared
Like some fierce loophole in a thunder cloud
Through which the red pelt of the lightning glared.

Then rose the huge, dark ocean in its pride,
Till, towering o'er its rocky bolts and bars,
It shook, in great, white smoke, its watery hide,
And toss'd its mane among the blackened stars.

While the dread winds gnawed off the mountain peaks,
And spat them down the steep, in deadly rain,
To play a thousand, murderous, midnight freaks
Among the trembling cities of the plain.

And the flushed lightning, stung with sudden ire,
Sprang like a burning tiger from its lair.
And seized the lone earth in its fangs of fire,
And shook it like a roebuck in the air.

As close upon its lurid heels there fell
The round, deep thunder, with appalling power,
That swung the low arched heavens like a bell,
And tolled through the abyss the funeral hour.

MIRAGE.

When early passion's deadly, flaming sword
  Drives manhood from the paradise of youth,
How altered all that once was so adored ;
  How robbed of all its innocence and truth.
The pathway leading, from our first bright hours
To where the future's last false mirage gleams,
Is strewn, at best, with but a few, pale flowers
  Whose fragrant breathings are but fitful dreams.

The blue-bell, nodding in the incensed dell,
  That once but simply told of heaven's own hue—
The opening rosebud, with its crimson spell,
  That seemed a mimic morning wet with dew,
No longer now retain their wonted dies,
  Or point to heaven or dawns first tinted streak,
One, trembles with the light of woman's eyes—
The other, with the beauties of her cheek.
Alas ! when once the fetters of the boy—
  Those blooming, rosy bonds—are torn apart,
Our bliss is changed into that fevered joy
  Whose burning pulses soon wear out the heart.

And, thus we wander, lingering. hoping yet,
  Until, at last, in darkness and in tears,
We find the star we sought so long, had set
Amid the brightness of our early years.

THE FIRST KISS.

In the first kiss she gives away
    She loses her own self in part,
And is another's from that day,
    Though e'en a change come o'er her heart.

Through weal or woe, through sun or shade,
    The sport of agony or bliss,
There stands the compact she has made,
    For she can ne'er recall that kiss.

DAWN.

With folded wings of dusky light
   Upon the purple hills she stands,
An angel between day and night,
   With tinted shadows in her hands—

Till suddenly transfigured there.
   With all her dazzling plumes unfurl'd,
She climbs the crimson-flooded air,
   And flies in glory o'er the world!

LINES.

INSCRIBED TO

HIS ROYAL HIGHNESS THE PRINCE OF WALES.

ON THE OCCASION OF HIS VISIT TO CANADA.

Not in the fierce, red glory of the battle field,
With angry laurels, dripping like the " crown of thorns,"
And smoking sinews knotted and twisted and wheeled
'Round every limb whose iron brawn both shield and
      buckler scorns,
Not thus descendest thou upon this peaceful shore,
Sung in by shot and shell, 'mid serried host on host
Whose murd'rous pulses surge and deadly thunders
      roar
Like dark November waves that rage along thy native
     coast.

Not thus ;—for, with o'erflowing hearts, we proudly
　　feel,
In thee Britannia clasps us closer to her breast,
Treading the waters, with pure apostolic zeal,
To shed her deeper radiance o'er the distant teeming
　　West,
That swift shall chase the desert like an April cloud,
And leave broad, golden valleys glowing in its stead :
Making its ancient, hoary silence ring aloud,
While quick'ning into life all that is cold, asleep or
　　dead.

Though thou dost come in youth, there's still around
　　thee shed
The broadest, brightest ray that glory ever cast,
Caught from thy Royal Mother's matchless heart and
　　head
That blaze with all the splendors of the Present and
　　the Past.
And this huge, shining link sublimely forged in thee,
And stretched in all Her love from kindred shore to
　　shore,
Shall shrivel to a span the blue gulf of the sea,
Till but one pulse throbs with our common life forever-
　　more.

No Creey here for thee need flash in bold relief,
The early pathway of thy greatness to illume ;
For thou can'st gather up a heavy golden sheaf
More precious far than was the blind Bohemian's fallen
      plume.
And thou shalt feel how strong—how wond'rous strong
      thou art
Ev'n in these out-works far beyond thy coming seas,
And that thou hast a citadel in every loyal heart,
Where thou can'st rest amid a thousand bloodless vic-
      tories.

For here are no strange people, swarthy, grim or wild.
To pour their feeble homage at thy gospel feet ;
But the sturdy Saxon and the fiery Celtic child
Hast'ning with cherished household words thine eager
      ear to greet.
And through our sunlit spaces and Cathedral woods
With mighty pillared aisles bannered with living green—
While shake our cities and our far-off solitudes—
Shall thundering roll a long God save thee, in
" God save the Queen."

" THE IRISH WOLF."

Some years ago, the London *Times* used the above epithet in designation of the Irish upon their native soil:—

SEEK music in the wolf's fierce howl
   Or pity in his blood-shot eye,
When hunger drives him out to prowl
   Beneath a rayless northern sky ;

But seek not that we should forgive
   The hand that strikes us to the heart,
And yet in mockery bids us live
   To count our stars as they depart.

We've fed the tyrant with our blood ;
   Won all his battles—built his throne—
Established him on land and flood,
   And sought his glory next our own.

We raised him from his low estate;
  We plucked his pagan soul from hell,
And led him pure to heaven's gate,
  Till he, for gold, like Judas, fell.

And when in one, long, soulless night,
  He lay unknown to wealth or fame.
We gave him empire—riches—light,
  And taught him how to spell his name.

But now ungenerous and unjust,
  Forgetful of our old renown,
He bows us to the very dust;
  But wears our jewels in his crown.

WHENE'ER I COME.

As when Aurora, glowing with the south,
  Strikes through the darkling grove in light and bloom,
So breaks in rapture from her jewelled mouth,
  The dazzling smile, half sunshine, half perfume.

Then, from its fragrant home of pearl and rose
  Her ever-tuneful tongue's flushed nightingale
In warbling silver, 'mid a thousand throes,
  Pours forth, once more, that burning fairy tale :—

"O, thou art come ! O, thou art come at last,
  To wake to ecstasy this love of ours ;
And call me back, from out the sainted past
  Where I've been twining wreaths of dreamy flowers."

"O, how I've gloated o'er that one loved name,
  With all my being—all my soul on fire,
Till turned to very ashes in the flame,
  Like some rapt Hindoo on her funeral pyre."

CLOUDS.

WET-NURSES of the flowers,
Come spread your wings between them and the sun,
Or they shall be undone
While passing through this waste of sultry hours.

Sweet odors on the plain
And drooping violets in yonder vale,
Are waiting, faint and pale,
To breathe afresh and scent the blessed rain.

Come laden then with showers,
And o'er the dusty hill and tangled mead
Scatter the shining seed,
That soon shall bloom, wet-nurses of the flowers.

THE CHURCH OF HUMANITY.

We cannot build it of the crumbling bones
    Quarried from the grim sepulchres of yore ;
Nor of the hollow, mythologic stones
    That shone so gaudily in classic lore;

We cannot fashion it of heads or creeds
    That parcel out our God before our face ;
But rather build it of the thoughts and deeds
    That purify and elevate our race.

Set its foundations deep in every zone.
    Its ritual, on every shining page,
Is love to God and love to man alone,
    And pity for the errors of the age.

Let its proud dome fill all the azure steep,
    And its vast chancels stretch from pole to pole ;
So that its mighty and majestic sweep
    Give ample space for every human soul.

IMPROMPTU—HER EYES.

Within those eyes both light and darkness beam,
Each in the rapture of its own extreme ;
So brightly dark and yet so darkly bright,
That we confound the shadow with the light.

OCEAN.

Awake, dark Ocean, in thy strength! My soul
    Loves the hoarse music of thy deep-mouthed bay;
Flash forth ye fires! ye mighty thunders roll!
    To me there's joy in every lurid ray,
    And every shout that swells the gathering fray
At which pale mortals in their anguish cower.
    Let me in adoration soar away
And join the glorious revel of the hour,
And mock at all that lives of human pomp and power!

Thy waters are earth's vanquishers alone;
    All that its millions fear thou dar'st defy;
No sovereignty thou knowest save thine own;
    Even Fire's red king,—before whom nations fly—
    And all his hosts howl in thy grasp and die;
Nor leave behind upon thy boundless zones,
    One trace to tell where they in darkness lie
Among thy nameless cities, fleets, and thrones—
Unfathom'd sepulchre of long lost empire's bones!

Should Time's vain sons in one wild tumult rush
   Down to thy shores, and with their mightiest cry
The tempest of thy voice essay to hush,
   And call thee downwards from that gloomy sky,
   'Twould be as though the sea-mew, passing by,
Had wail'd its feeble note upon the blast ;
   Even the fell winds their direst whoop shall try,
   And the deep crater bellow to the last,—
Thou can'st out-shout them all—dread conqueror of the
   past !

I kneel !—thou art in audience with thy God,
   In the dark palace of the thunder cloud !
Thou art called forth ; and at His awful nod
   Upwards thou rollest ; while the mysterious crowd,
   That, in mail'd splendor, thy dim depths enshroud,
Each impulse in their coral caverns share,
   And own, in silence, that thou now art bow'd
Before Him, in the regions of the air,
And, that sublimely heaving, thou dost worship there !

IDYL.

Morning stands in the gates of the East,
With a single star pinned in the night of her hair
That's thrown back till her bosom and brow are as bare
    As if draped but to gladden a feast ;
While her eye and her cheek, flashing gloriously there,
Flood with purple and crimson the tremulous air
    As the wine floods and flushes a feast.

Now, the landscape is set to the music of June,
And the breezes and streamlets and bees are in tune ;
While the full-throated warblers that haunt the cool
     bowers,
Chant their matins aloud in the bright, purple hours,
And the ruby-flecked tenants that people the brook
Are yet unallured by the treacherous hook ;
While the wild-bird, in nooks that are silent and lone,
Sits as still on her nest as if sculptured in stone.

See the steed, that arose at the first peep of dawn,
Shake the dew from his coat on the sweet-scented lawn,
And the milkmaid, that gathers the kine round her pail,
Add the rose on her cheek to the rose of the vale ;
While the flowers at her feet, in most exquisite bloom,
Pour abroad on the air all their richest perfume,
And the husbandman tends the green blades on the
    wold,
That shall yet glow around him in ridges of gold.

TO MUSIC.

WHAT name O Music, lov'st thou best—
　 "Sweet foretaste of the joys above;"
"Seraphic language of the blest;
Or soul of feeling, soul of love;"?
Dear mistress of my spirit's tone,
These all are thine—and thine alone.

When softly o'er my list'ning ear,
Thy magic's mellow whisp'rings steal,
That spirit trembling in a tear,
To every dying note could kneel,
And wish 'twere from this chain unbound,
To bear it to the heaven of sound.

AMEN !

(1864.)

God of the bleeding North and South,
   Restore their mangled brotherhood,
Who now, before the cannon's mouth,
   Lie weltering in each other's blood.

They are the children of one sire,
   And both have claims alike on Thee ;
Then, stay the work of sword and fire,
   And let the freedmen still be free.

Oh ! listen while the nations plead—
   Who, too, have reaped the bitter yield,
And frightful harvests that succeed
   The red rain of the battle field

And curb the anger and the pride
  Now blindly struggling, hand to hand ;
And, in thy pity, turn aside
  The flood that darkly sweeps the land.

If blood did e'er from sin release
  A people of one common flesh,
They, in the white-robed arts of peace,
  Have offered up a Christ afresh.

Oh ! stay the awful tempest, then,
  And let the glory of Thy face
Break through the darkness, once again,
  Upon this brave, misguided race.

SONG.

Come to me, idle wind,
Come to me—sing to me;
Come from my waking flower,
And her sweets bring to me;
Come from her dewy bower,
And, when you're coming,
Bring me the early song that she is humming.
Come to me, idle wind,
Come to me—sing to me;
Come from her dewy bower,
And its sweets bring to me.

Fly to me idle wind,
Fly to me—sing to me;
Fly from her couch of balm,
And its sweets bring to me;
Fly when she slumbers calm.
And, when you're flying,
Bring me the name that you hear her half sighing.
Fly to me, idle wind,
Fly to me—sing to me;
Fly from her couch of balm,
And its sweets bring to me.

ADDRESS.

Spoken by Miss Cora Jefferson at the opening of the first Museum and Opera House, Buffalo, N. Y

In this fair land of genius, every hour
Lends some bright feature to the busy age,
And clothes the bar, the pulpit and the stage—
That classic triad—with new pomp and power;
'Till Virtue, Truth and Pleasure, all combined,
Alike enchant and elevate the mind.

Yes, here, where Freedom's whitest flag's unfurl'd
Beneath the purple of the purest skies,
New altars and new domes to them arise—
The glory and the envy of the world;
And we would humbly follow in the train,
And to the list add yet another Fane.

And what more genial site could one divine
Than this, so gently sloping from yon wave,
Where throng to-night the beauteous and the brave
Whose virtues through their faults and foibles shine—
Where trade and commerce flourish hand in hand,
And peace and plenty bless the teeming land.

And where, while struggling in life's mighty van,
The noblest aspirations fire the mind,
And—the most human of the human kind—
Man seeks to elevate his fellow man,
And wreathe his honored country's glowing name
With every laurel known to wealth and fame.

And what a pleasing mission shall be ours ;
For, now that heaven has wiped away our tears,
And into ploughshares beaten all our spears,
We'd strew the path of youth and age with flowers ;
Nor leave one thorn concealed amid the bloom
To wound the feet that they should but perfume.

Then boldly on your aid we shall rely ;
For, know that we but ask it on the part
Of Nature and her dumb twin sister, Art,
And all that charms the ear or lights the eye,
As well as every subtle, inward sense
That owns the power of silent eloquence.

And thus, sustained by your approving smiles,
This temple of the Muses yet shall stand
A sculptured pillar in this favored land ;

While its fair priestess with her gracious wiles,
Shall place it on that eminence sublime
Where not one other step remains to climb.

So, now, kind friends, as he may read who runs,
Long, long be yours prosperity and health,
And long, long live this glorious Commonwealth
With all its recent brave, historic sons,
And this proud mart—but, hark !—The prompter's bell !
Ladies and gentlemen,—a brief farewell.

SWALLOWS.

Like shining shuttles, weaving the bright spring,
  See how they flash throughout the balmy air,
Whose sunny warp and woof symphonious ring
  To their gay twitter, and their swift wing there.

Or see them dip into the silvery stream,
  And, dripping, shoot athwart the crimson west,
Till, in its deepening glow, the spray drops seem
  Some beam of evening pow'dered on their breast.

But something far more dear these sports foretell——
  The scented mead, the grove, the bee, the flower,
And the flushed lover hastening down the dell,
  To merge all sunshine in one twilight hour—

To taste the dew that's tinged with pearl and rose,
  And whisper softly, mid the trembling leaves,
To some one sighing gently, as she goes,
  "Oh, would, the swallows never left our eaves."

THE QUANDARY.

CALL it not noon, false skies, it can't be noon :
She slumbers, and we need not look for light ;
For while those eyes are closed it must be night :
    And who shall kiss them out of the sweet swoon ?

And would'st thou call it dawn should they ope now,
Pleading such lustre as is hidden there ;
Surely, false skies, the earth could never bear
    The light of two such mornings on its brow.

But night or day may still glide on apace ;
For if in soft repose she slumbers yet ;
The shadow of the radiance that is set
    Divinely plays about her sainted face.

Then say, where lies this strange, enchanting spell—
In her bright opening orbs or slumbers calm,
Or her sweet lips that flush their own sweet balm
    For I am sore perplexed, and cannot tell ?

THE FATAL CAPE.

Around her rayless path the dark fog lay,
As though the dull, cold air were thick with crape;
While through the deepening gloom she gropes her
      way—
A funeral ship——along that fatal cape.

And, though her iron bulk seems tried and true,
And twice two hundred souls in her have faith,
A weird silence reigns among the crew,
That seems the **presage** of approaching death.

That crash! O, God, she strikes a sunken rock!
And never shall she plough the waves again!
A long, wild cry accompanies the shock,
And all the sea is filled with drowning men!

With a pale throng the latest boat has gone—
Escaping swiftly, and in dire alarm,
From the mad swimmers, sinking one by one,
Till disappears the last uplifted arm!

THE VESPER HYMN.

Amid the purple sunset hours,
  Humming like an angel's wing,
Within a nook of wayside flowers,
  A little child began to sing.

At first her voice was almost mute—
  A sort of soft, melodious hush ;
But soon it broke into a lute,
  To emulate a neighboring thrush.

As though the song of seraphim
  Came gushing from the upper spheres,
Then rose a wondrous vesper hymn
  Upon my eager, ravished ears ;

And as the concert grew apace,
  And child and bird sang out amain,
The sun poured on her upturned face
  A glory like to golden rain.

While in the glow of parting day,
  The warbler shook his shining throat,
As if new raptures fired the lay
  He heard repeated note for note.

And when at last the magic song
  Was o'er, and child and bird grew dim,
I thought, with saddened heart, how long
  Since I had sung *my* vesper hymn.

FEBRUARY.

THE famished sun crawls through a flaw in night,
   And blurs the hissing tempest into morn,
Spreading a misty pool of sickly light
   That widens till the ghastly day is born.

And lonely trees, on uplands, blown as bare
   As beggars on the hills when winds are out,
Stagger, like drunken giants, in the air,
   And wildly toss their naked arms about.

The ocean, agonized with winds, and sleets
   That pave an angry pathway down from heaven,
Thunders and smokes among the shattered fleets
   That, like dead sea fowl, on the rocks are driven.

And the bright river, with its deep-toned lute,
   And brook, that sang amid the flowery wild,
Beneath an icy slab, dark, drear and mute,
   Lie side by side—dead mother and dead child.

And, now, the blue-lipped orphan treads the street,
  With naked shoulders pressed against her ears,
Washing the red stains from her bleeding feet,
  At every trembling pause, with bitter tears.

While, 'mid the gloomy waste that 'round her lies,
  Nor sight nor sound to cheer her can she trace ;
For the dumb earth, before her sunken eyes,
  A huge, chill ball of anguish rolls through space.

AT LAST! AT LAST!

THE smouldering heavens have fallen upon the plain ;
  And through the haze the drowsy, hot wind flows,
Till there is but a dark and sultry stain
  Where stood the crimson glory of the rose.

No playful pinion fans the empty sky ;
  The song within the languid grove is done,
And drooping lilies like dead maidens lie
  In the red war-path of the Indian sun.

The wayside shrub in vain holds out its hands ;
  The panting kine creep close beneath the hill ;
And in the dell the cottage maiden stands,
  A thirsty angel near an empty rill.

But see !—at last along the burning capes
  That stretch their dusty limbs upon the sea,
The Christed shower among the famished grapes,
  Performs again the feat of Galilee !

And touches with a myriad silvery wands
  The poor parched flowers that strew the voiceless
      earth,
Till, bursting from their soiled and weary bonds
  Each starts, a phœnix, into second birth.

And Nature's soul becomes attuned once more,
  Till gazing on the apostolic trair
.That sweeps the sky, we almost could adore
  The clouds that preach the gospel of the rain.

SONG.

I ASK no joys but those you give—
　　No joys but those you share;
No lips but yours to bid me live;
　　No smiles but those they wear.

No morn but what o'erspreads your cheek;
　　No light but from your eye;
No music, love, but what you speak;
　　No language but your sigh.

No pillow, darling, but your breast;
　　No curtain but your hair,
To fall in clouds around my rest,
　　And shade my rapture there.

CHRISTMAS.

Ring out ! ring out! sweet Christmas chimes,
   The Yule log roars upon the hearth,
We would recall the good old times,
   When all the land was filled with mirth.

Once more upon the wings of time
   Your happy freaks and frolics bring,
And let your notes blend with the rime,
   That's wrought by our gray Northern King.

His gems float through the morning air,
   Like diamonds broken in the light,
And strown the landscape everywhere
   With all the radiance of his white.

And from the shining, icy floor,
  Where youth and beauty glide along,
We hear repeated, o'er and o'er,
  The joyous laugh and joyous song.

Ring out! nor e'er a moment pause;
  Let all be gay, around, above,
For we all wait some Santa Claus,
  To meet us in the way we love.

OUR WORK.

Good people, quit your weary knees,
    Your drowsy prayers and useless sighs,
And leap up to your feet and seize
    The present moment as it flies.

God fixed the destiny of men,
    From the first hour that saw their birth,
A brawny arm and tongue and pen,
    To deal alike with heaven and earth.

We want no maudlin, lazy crowds,
    With lengthened face and upturned eye,
Communing with the empty clouds
    That float above them two miles high.

An honest heart and sturdy hand,
    These are the implements we want
To till the heart and till the land,
    Instead of all this wretched cant.

Those who aright would worship God,
   Must leave a record of their creed
Upon the expectant soul and sod,
   In sowing both with proper seed.

And when the work's securely done
   Within the heart and on the plain,
No fear but He'll supply the sun,
   No fear but He'll supply the rain.

THE ANGEL OF THE BROOK.

SWEET angel of the brook whose snowy wings,
That drip, from morn till night, with shining spray,
Are ever trembling o'er these lips of mine
And filling with pure nectar, day by day,
The crystal cup that I would fill with wine
As madly I'd forsake the sparkling springs
That laugh and sport through many a sylvan nook,
     Sweet angel of the brook.

I'll taste no deep stained fount where rubies burn,
But the bright stream that leaps the jewelled crag,
And hangs its dazzling curtain in the air,
While, safe at last, the weary, sunset stag,
Tangled with rainbows that entwine him there,
Drinks the cool silver from thy rocky urn ;
There shall I pledge thee, with one long, fond look,
     Sweet angel of the brook.

HER TONGUE.

There dwells a crimson nightingale
  Within a cage of pearl and rose
Through whose bright bars a burning tale
  Of love and passion ever flows.

And I so cherish the sweet lay
  That, filled with perfume, 'round me pours,
Whenever it would die away,
  I fly and kiss the prison doors.

THE WOODS.

THE mourning woods now bare their aching breast,
  And wildly toss their naked arms on high
O'er the last shreds of their autumnal vest
  That float in eddies through the cold, bleak sky.

The sear earth wraps its sackcloth round their feet,
  And snows like ashes fall upon their head,
While many a bitter tear of cutting sleet
  Is darkly o'er the leafless ruin shed.

And the chill fingers of the wintry blast
O'er their wild harp-strings are in sadness swept,
  Till one might feel the beauties of the past
Lay not unsung, unhonored, and unwept.

THE BEWILDERED RIVER.

Oh, river! river! on thy shining way
    Thou never yet hast seen a morn so fair;
For on thee pours a more celestial ray
    Than thou canst calmly bear.

This blue dawn might have longer slept in night,
    For thou would'st not have missed it from the skies,
      While travelling onward in the wondrous light
        Of those dark, lustrous eyes——

Those liquid orbs whose all-pervading glow
    Might touch thy coldest waves with fond desire,
And bathe thy silvery tenants far below
    In mellow, crystal fire—

Might bathe them in strange glory, till they flew
    From out thy breast in sportive jets of flame,
Seeking, so strange, the splendor of their hue,
    The source from whence it came.

But thou art sore bewildered in the blaze
   That now doth light thee downwards to the main;
For not a single drop touched by those rays
   Shall e'er be dark again.

And, when they're scattered wide on distant strands
   So pure a lustre still shall cling to them,
That wanderers oft shall stoop, with eager hands,
   To clutch some fancied gem.

THE POET.

'Mid the pale ashes of his dreamy face,
  The embers of his eyes begin to glow ;
His gorgeous livery waits in empty space,
  With eager pulses flashing to and fro.

Breathless he mounts his flaming chariot now,
  And, like the prophet, swift is heavenwards
    rolled,
Till the shekinah burns upon his brow,
  With lustre that would blind the priests of old.

But, soon he will descend with living bread
  For the proud, thoughtless beggars of our race ;
And, with unheeded glories round his head,
  Resume, once more, his weary leaden pace.

EYES.

Oh Beauty !—thou magical skeleton case,
In thy brow two of God's living jewels are set
As soul-stars, to guide the lost ones of our race,
Who are strangers to heaven and happiness yet.

But thy eloquent beacon too seldom appears
Flashing faithfully down on the wanderer's feet ;
Or endeavoring to beam through a deluge of tears,
In the gloom where Affliction and Misery meet.

Yet, alas ! on each folly that secretly twines
A bright, beautiful serpent around us so fast,
From the depths of its treasure, the mellow light shines,
'Till the gaze of the monster is on us at last.

And we wander through life, like a phantom unblest,
As we struggle, in vain, to shake off his control ;
'Till the last ray of hope flickers out in our breast,
And we die, with his fangs buried deep in our soul.

Oh! then, while the spoiler relentlessly preys
On the flowerets and fruits of the heart's purest bloom,
Shall the banquet be treach'rously lit by the rays
That were kindled by heav'n to avert such a doom?

Oh, never!—those gems shall not shine at the feast,
Nor illumine the paths by the prodigal trod;
But forever blaze forth, like the star in the East,
That once led the Chaldee to the feet of his God.

"TEE WEET."

I heard the lonely piping of a bird,
When the cold April shower hung on his wing;
And all the depths within my soul were stirred
While listening to the poor, dejected thing,
As he sat in the melancholy sleet
Wailing in trembling tones, "tee weet, tee weet."

All night he lay out in the frozen moon,
Upon a barren branch against the skies;
Mocked by a thousand gleams of leafy June,
The moment that he closed his weary eyes;
And ever gathering up his chilly feet,
While whispering dreamily, "tee weet, tee weet."

At sunrise when aroused from his unrest,
He shook his plumes and tried a happier note;
But the faint music died within his breast,
Before he e'en could pour it from his throat;
And drearily, he only could repeat
The same forlorn refrain, "tee weet, tee weet."

Alas ! he had begun too soon to rove ;
And vainly now the folly he deplores,
That lured him from the fragrant orange grove,
To meet the tardy spring upon our shores,
And left him in that desolate retreat
Piping from morn till night, "tee weet, tee weet."

THE MAGIC MIRROR.

Beside a brook that danced in silvery whirls
  Down through a dell that caught its sparkling tone,
As playfully it threw a string of pearls
  Around the neck of many a mossy stone,
There paused the sweetest of all little girls
  That had been wandering in the wood alone ;

For where the wild blooms, in the morning beam,
  In thickest clusters hung above her head,
Within a pool, that stole from out a stream
  And at her feet a shining mirror spread,
She saw a laughing child as in a dream,
  Laden with fragrant blossoms, white and red.

One sultry noon again she wandered there,
  And soon beside the pool abstracted stood,
Gazing upon a vision, bright and fair,
  In the first fervid flush of womanhood,
With dreamy, purple eyes. and golden hair—
  Soft eyes that pensive looked from out the flood.

And once again she came, at close of day,
  And peered into the waters as of yore;
But now she only saw—bent, old, and gray,—
  A palsied form, with features furrowed o'er;
And, taking one last look, she turned away,
  And to the magic mirror came no more.

"THE VISITOR."

Though stretched upon my dungeon floor,
I knew a light came to the door—
A far-off door, in iron mail,
Hewn from a frowning mass of oak
 On which had rung the thunder stroke
Three hundred years without avail—
But then, that light, so sad and pale,
Could not, alas ! an entrance win,
The jailer would not let HER in.

Then lonely turning to the stars
I felt sweet odors through my bars—
Curst bars that grin upon my gloom ;
Foul, murderous bludgeons swung on high
To brain the daylight in the sky,
And weld me down within my tomb—
But, then, that rosy-lipped perfume,
Soon sobbed itself away and died :
The jailer pushed HER steps aside.

But, mark!—ere long, a golden flood
Swept oe'r my sense, and, lo! she stood
Fast locked within my fond embrace.
She! radiant in her raven hair,
With loveliness I scarce could bear;
Such varied beauties could I trace
In her voluptuous form and face.
While now, in turn—how strange to say!
She kept the jailer out till day!

LINES.

Tho' the heart may be sad, when the brow is o'ercast
By some shadow that falls from a dream of the past,
There's a magical power in the gloom that it brings,
That can only awaken those deepest toned strings.

When the isles of the deep, in the far sunset sky,
Steal in crimson and gold on the wanderer's eye,
'Tis the flushed ray of eve lends the beautiful gleam,
And distance that mellows them down to a dream.

And when mem'ry would trace on our bright youthful
    years,
The wreck of our smiles in the light of our tears,
The pencil is dipt in the sunset of age ;
And time sheds that soft hallow'd beam o'er the page.

"TOTTY."

I'VE a sweet, little darling on whom we all dote,
Who is hovering about me from morning till night,
With a hug or a kiss, or a pluck at my coat,
While her innocent heart bubbles up with delight.

And when trying to catch her, she oft from me glides
Like a sunbeam that shadows chase over the floor ;
But I know where the bright, little rattle-brain hides,
For I hear her soft laughter behind the room door.

Then, I steal off on tip-toe, and soon find her out ;
Though she thinks herself safe with her face to the wall,
'Till I toss all her brown, silken tresses about,
While her silver-strung voice like a lute fills the hall.

Then she bounds to my bosom, and kiss upon kiss
Is so rapidly showered on my forehead and cheek,
That, o'ercome by a love so spontaneous as this,
I oft hobble away, scarcely able to speak.

And whene'er through the past I in memory roam,
Some odd prank, at my knee, brings me back with
    surprise,
To perceive, after all, I'm not sad or from home,
But just dancing within the blue depths of her eyes.

JOUSSEF'S SOLILOQUY IN THE STORM.

FROM AN UNPUBLISHED POEM.

Now, tell of the bright gem, ethereal born,
That flashes on the brow of the young Morn,
When naked from her jewelled couch she steals,
And, blushing, all the charms of light reveals ;
While through the diamond balm of her repose
Each rosy-tinted feature brighter glows,
Till, won by warmer light, she glides away
And melts into the fervid arms of Day.

And tell us that the Moon, in pearly dreams,
Among the matted locks of Darkness gleams
Pale as tired sunbeams that had wandered far
And sunk to rest upon some distant star.
Tell how her dewy fingers, soft and white,
Weave all the mystic glories of the night,
And loose, with magic touch, the silvery springs
That gush out o'er the Shadow-Spirit's wings.

But what are these ?—mere tinsel—childish fires
Such as the poet's soul of flame admires
But cannot worship.   Others may adore
A ray serenely pure but nothing more—
May breathe the incense of the closing flower,
And drain its cup of the ambrosial shower,
Drink in the morn, or tracing moonlit streams.
Dream by the lake they nurse, the dream of dreams.

But he of that sublimely kindled eye,
Kneels not to the pale glowworms of the sky ;
Nor from the tinted fount of opening day
Wins the undying radiance of that ray ;
Unmoved by these, alone he ceaseless broods
O'er Nature in her mighty solitudes,
Unlocks the volume sealed to vulgar crowds,
And lost amid the ocean or the clouds,
Bending in silent awe his misty form
Drinks in the inspiration of the storm !

There, as the deafening thunders o'er him roll,
The energies of his exulting soul
Burst forth in all their vigor ; and he feels
The thrill that beggars language, but reveals

Man's immortality—the living thought
That sets the trammels of the flesh at naught
And fearless, on undying wing explores
The desert far beneath the sea, or soars
Beyond all height, nor staggers on its way
Till blazing in the dread, eternal ray
That, blasting all created being's sight,
Seals up the source of uncreated light.

Unfathomable secret, deepening still,
Whose touch creative sent that living thrill
Through primal darkness till the bonds of day—
The floodgates of primeval light—gave way,
And down the steep a shining torrent rolled
To curtain evening with its mellow gold
And spread the azure of the morning sky.
Tell us, a spark of thine own essence why
Pent up within these perishable veins,
Boasting of its divinity in chains
From which an angry wasp could set it free :
What splendid shackles for a deity !
The mystery's thine, O God !   Thy power is there ;
And he who'd madly thus the secret dare,
Forgets that Thou alone can'st understand
Man, the proud work of Thy almighty Hand.

And bare the union of his two-fold birth—
The purity of heaven and dross of earth
Combined to meet Thy will—Forgets to Thee
The locks of Strength are shorn eternally,
Forgets, the rocky ridge the globe that spans
And the frail gossamer the zephyr fans,
Alike are strong or feeble in thy sight,
The one not heavy, nor the other light.

MORN.

Peeping through her purple bars,
Down an endless street of stars,
Melting all the ingots up,
　　As her eyes more brightly shine,
Morning in a crystal cup
　　Floats the bubble earth in wine.

From the red lips of the sea,
Out into immensity,
Steals a tongue of green and gold
　　Soon to swarm with giddy flies,
When the mighty landscape's rolled
　　Farther to the western skies.

Splendor now by splendors quaffed,
Deeper grows at every draught,
　　Till the monogram of fire—
The round red llanos of the sun—
　　Fills with flame the heavens entire,
And sweeps all glories into one.

RESURGAM !

Come ! let us form a solid square,
    No matter what our creed or clan,
And plant our drooping standard there,
    Beside some wounded Dalgais* man,

'Till all its emerald folds unfurled
    O'er yonder sea of kindred sheen,
Shall mid-way meet before the world,
    Its other half of living green.

Then shall a rainbow span the skies—
    A pledge of countless glorious years—
The light of a young nation's eyes
    That flashes through her joyous tears.

While in his ancient glory decked
    Beneath the arch of dazzling rays,
The haughty Celt shall stand erect.
    As once he stood in other days.

* The Dalgais were the favorite troops of Brian Borrombhe, or Boru, who, when wounded in fight and unable to stand, requested that they should be lashed to a stake planted by the side of a sound man, so as they might still do battle.

THE "BRIDGE OF SIGHS."*

Make way for the iron horse that with might and main
Comes neighing, and clanking, and thundering over the
      plain,
Till the air grows hot with his furious chariot wheels,
As they grind and spin, and leap at his smoking
      heels !

He is proud to-day, for he knows he bears along,
In all his matchless strength, a numerous, happy throng,
The gentle and the brave, and men who won pure gold,
And dark-eyed loveliness with its own wealth untold.

But list ! his loud neigh, seems a strange, long fiendish
      scream ;
And with so deep a roar he draws his breath of steam,
That the dark fireman mounts high on his dusky back
To look out, for himself, along the distant track.

* Scene of the terrible railway accident of 1857 at the Desjardin
Canal between Hamilton and Toronto, Canada.

But who cares for his breath?—Or who cares for his
    neigh?
With half the lightning's speed he travels on his way,
And grinds down the strong rails, with his broad,
    ponderous tire,
Till they crack and smoke beneath him like unto bars
    of fire.

Let him then, into wilder swiftness madly wrought,
Sweep through cleft mountains and through valleys,
    swift as thought,
Till the tall, telegraphic, spectral, wire-bound posts
Flash by him in a flight of strange, gaunt, wooden
    ghosts.

There can't be danger now, as on he flies apace ;
For lynx-eyed men are near to guide him in the race ;
And when they reach yon bridge that's stretched out in
    the air,
How gallantly, you'll see, he'll cross the gulf that's
    there.

The dark-eyed one now dreams of all she loves on
    earth ;
And the sweet child laughs loud in its own sinless
    mirth ;

And the gay youth is counting over his years to come ;
And the men of gold are plotting, in a deep, low hum.

But, God of pity, see ! the bridge they now would
  sweep,
Gives way, and the whole train leaps down the awful
  steep !
Leaps down into the shuddering, gloomy gulf below,
Crashing and thundering mid its shattered ice, and
  snow !

The dark-eyed one's hot brains spurt through her raven
  hair ;
And the limbs of the men of gold are scattered everywhere ;
And the hopeful youth is nothing but a pulpy mass ;
And the poor dead child stares out through eyes of
  strange, smoked glass.

Oh, God ! who built that bridge — that fatal bridge of
  sighs ?—
Who placed the pitfall there, before our very eyes ?
Was it some railway-man who, in his sordid strife,
Thought more of a piece of gold than he thought of a
  brother's life ?

THE SPIRIT OF LIGHT.

Morn ! Morn on the hills !—how entranced we behold
The first steps of the beautiful spirit of light,
As she opens her long silken lashes of night,
And shakes out her tresses of purple and gold
On the glittering crags of yon perilous height
That erst in the gray mist slept cheerless and cold.

So gorgeous her ray on the lark's dewy breast,
As he sings her his song in the azure afar,
That the shepherd boy, gazing, oft thinks him a star
Sinking into its calm crystal bosom to rest ;
Till o'ercome by the blaze that encircles her car,
He descends, once again, to his low grassy nest.

She awakens the flowers from their odorous dreams,
Brightly gem'd with the spray of the ocean of heaven,
To catch the rich dyes that were blotted at even,
When shadows crept in on their banquet of beams,
And stole from their cheeks the deep tinge it had given,
And flooded the landscape with cold, rayless streams.

IMAGE EVALUATION
TEST TARGET (MT-3)

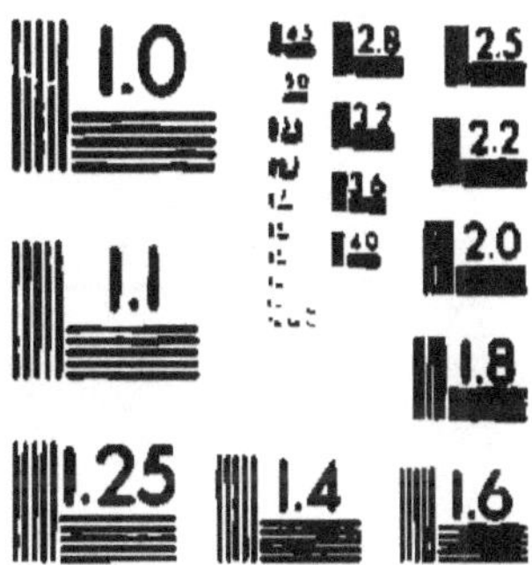

And joyously now, in her sunny-eyed glee,
Her rosy-tipp'd fingers she points towards the glade,
In the face of the Ethiop spectre of shade,
Whose dusky brow pales as he hastens to flee
To those solitudes where, in his dark cowl arrayed,
He can crouch at the foot of some huge spreading tree.

AUTUMN-SONG.

The heavens have dropped in showers of gold,
   Upon the bright Danæan fields ;
And up the east the sun is rolled,
   In all the light his glory yields.
Then brothers let us haste away,
And seize the treasures while we may.

With harmless jest and happy song,
   We'll lay the full sheaves at our feet ;
And ply our task the whole day long,
   Unmindful of the fervid heat.
And when the failing light gets dim,
We'll pause and chaunt our evening hymn.

THE GRAY LINNET.

THERE's a little gray friar in yonder green bush,
Clothed in sackcloth—a little gray friar
Like a druid of old in his temple— but hush !
He's at vespers ; you must not go nigher.

Yet, the rogue! can those strains be addressed to the
      skies,
And around us so wantonly float,
Till the glowing refrain like a shining thread flies
From the silvery reel of his throat ?

When he roves though he stains not his path through
      the air
With the splendor of tropical wings,
All the lustre denied to his russet plumes there,
Flashes forth through his lay when he sings ;

For the little gray friar is so wonderous wise,
Though in such a plain garb he appears,
That on finding he can't reach your soul through your
    eyes,
He steals in through the gates of your ears.

But the cheat!—tis not heaven he's warbling about—
Other passions, less holy, betide—
For, behold! there's a little gray nun peeping out
From a bunch of green leaves at his side.

ASSORTED GEMS.

WHEN freighted with those sparkling, primrose-stars
  That thickly strew the purple fields of heaven,
At eve the murmuring waves in silvery cars
  Are gently shorewards by the zephyrs driven.

There, as they troop along their seashell-road,
  An angel, from her woodbine cot descending,
Shall add the brightest jewels to their load,
  While o'er them, with her rustic pitcher, bending.

TO BACCHUS.

As did the Olympian Thunderer's last embrace,
In ashes lay thy Bœotian mother's charms,
So, now, from age to age, the human race
Lies crushed, to dust, within thy iron arms.

O'er every land and tongue thy spell is cast;
And Fame, herself, while blushing for our sires,
Owns that a thousand glories of the past,
Caught half their lustre from thy wanton fires.

Tear from thy brow that sunny wreath—false god,
To thee belongs no leaf of vernal bloom ;
Thy vintage from the broken heart is trod,
And thou should'st wear the emblem of the tomb.

Unmask, and let the votary of the bowl,
Feel, for a moment, all thy dark deceit ;—
Fear not—he'll clasp thee closer to his soul,
And live and die a leper at thy feet.

EVENING.

With glowing hand, along the purple west
Now, evening strews the golden wreck of day,
And gathers from the ocean's trembling breast
The mellow fragments of its parting ray,
As slowly dies amid the deep'ning shades,
The latest spark that struggles with their gloom,
The landscape in the lovely ruin fades,
And earth's half plunged within her ancient tomb.

O, light ! thou shadow of the Great Unknown,
That fell o'er shapeless worlds, ere starry skies
Were wrapt in shining folds, around His Throne,
To hide its majesty from mortal eyes,
Thou now art fled, but not forever past,
Another day shall of thy glory born,
Close just as sweetly as now clos'd the last,
And 'wake as fair, as blue, as bright a morn.

TEAR ME FROM HER?

Didst thou but know how deep this love of mine,
And how each eager moment of my life,
My very soul, I round her shadow twine,
Thou soon would'st cease this vain—this cruel strife.

Yon giant oak in all its towering pride
Up by the roots, perchance thou mightest tear ;
But never cans't thou move me from her side
So strongly—deeply am I rooted there.

What !—tear me from those beaming eyes away,
Till into gloom the direst I am hurled ?
What ! lock me up, in the broad face of day,
In the dark chambers of a rayless world ?

Ah ! no, my life, my light and all were fled,
Shouldst thou remove me from her glowing sphere ;
For when I leave her bosom now, I'm dead,
And must retrace my steps to feel I'm here.

.

SONG.

Roses white and roses red,
  Heavy with dew,
Let me whisper what they've said,
  My love, of you.

One said, "like me she's ruby bright,"
  The other, "like me, fair ;"
But both said, trembling with delight,
  "Oh ! twine us with her hair ;

Or let us breathe her summer sigh,
  And all her beauty share,
As on her snowy breast we lie
  And gather fragrance there."

Roses white and roses red,
  Dripping with dew,
This, my love, is what they said
  Of you !—of you !

FOUND DROWNED!

Come nearer! Come nearer, I say:
Why shrink from her now that she's dead?
  What have you to fear from her more?
  Her faults and her follies are o'er:
This white-limb'd atonement has wash'd them away
Like the wavelet that laps the dark hair 'round her head
  And sighs her along to the shore.
  What have you to fear from her more?
Come nearer! come nearer, I say.

Of her failings—hold !—breathe not a breath !
The curtain has fall'n on the past ;
  Not a vestige of sin can you trace
  In the beautiful stone of that face
So calm and surpassingly sculptured in death.
Poor, lone, weary thing, she is holy, at last—
  Neither sorrow nor sin can efface
  The beautiful stone of that face.
Of her failings—hold !—breathe not a breath.

See the sands of her silvery shroud
Shine like stars through the night of her hair ;
 Bend o'er her,—perhaps they were given
 As she stole towards the threshold of heaven,
To sprinkle with light the dark depths of the cloud
That o'ershadowed the hope that the lost one was there.
 Bend o'er her, the darkness is riven ;
 She has stol'n o'er the threshold of heaven—
See the stars of her silvery shroud !

THANKSGIVING.

Now Autumn like some milk-white ox of old,
Has trodden out her heavy sheaves of gold
Upon the broad floor of the teaming earth;
Then let us mingle with our joyous mirth
Words of far purer import than are those
At which the fervid cheek of passion glows,
And raise a song of heartfelt praise to Him
Who filled his children's store house to the brim.

TO THE SEA.

Unfathomable waste of winds and waves,
And stars that tuft the purple woof of night
And pin it shadowed down amid thy depths,
How great art thou in all thy twofold strength !
Whether one vast unbroken sheet of calm
Where the long finger of the lonely mast
Points through the azure solitude, to God !
Or whether from out thy solemn slumbers roused,
Shaking thy dripping hide and awful crest,
Thou goest forth to meet the fierce typhoon
That, plumed with darkness, blur'd with fire and flame
Scatters thy fleets 'mid shoals and sunken rocks,
And leaves them in dark fragments drifting there !

How great art thou at morn, or noon, or eve
When through the crimson portals of the West
The huge, red furnace of the dying day
Pours out its lava o'er thy radiant floor,
Till thou art as the vestibule of heaven
Leading to the great drop-scene of the sun

That curtains the dread space before His Throne,
And till the earth clasped in thy glowing arms
In emerald splendor's borne along its path
And thou dost seem a giant ruby set
In the broad chasing of a thousand shores
Where thou dost meet the sea-shells and the sands—
A rim of golden dust, and pearl and rose.

TOO LATE.

STILL painfully—still painfully she sung
Like a bee tangled in a honied flower
Where he had all day long in revel hung
'Till drunk with nectar, at the evening hour
He tried in vain his drooping pinions' power,
And sought to wheel—as erst he used to roam—
Along a sunbeam to his amber home.

A vulture sat within her burning eyes,
Whene'er they told her she had been beguiled ;
And wildly gathering up the broken ties,
She'd link them while she gazed upon her child ;
Until in white-lipped agony she smiled,
And, with her anguish pouring o'er the brim,
Would still believe that she was all to him.

Her hope was like a wounded bird that springs
Up through the darkness and the tempest's din,
And sweeps a shining desert, with his wings,
Above the clouds that shut his eyrie in,
Until at last his brain begins to spin,
And wearied, down he slowly sinks again
Lone, dark and prostrate on the gloomy plain.

THE CYNOSURE.

This world of ours is never dark,
  If there is but one little star
To cheer us and to guide our bark,
  Or near or far.

And though, to less inquiring eyes,
  It may be clad in feeble rays,
It sheds, within our waste of skies,
  A solar blaze.

But when dark shadows round it throng
  Though all the heavens be filled with day,
How blindly do we grope along
  Our ruined way.

EVER WITH THEE.

WHEN, love, I for a moment from thee part,
Think'st thou that for that moment I am free?
A silver cord within my beating heart
I but unwind and leave the end with thee.

So as that in my strangest, fiercest flight,
I but in narrowing circles round thee soar,
Till faint with absence at thy feet I light
And nestle in that balmy breast once more.

AUTUMN.

THE ripe fields are scattered in eddies of gold
On the verge of the forest that's kindling apace ;
And the orchards that dapple the wide-spreading wold,
Through their loopholes of leaves—as we pause to be-
    hold—
Flash their beautiful, festival lamps in our face.

And the amber-coned pear, with the peach's flushed
    ball,
And the sunny-cheeked apple that's crimsoned all o'er,
Blend with pleiads of grapes that in purple showers
    fall
Over many a green-muffled trellis and wall,
With a 'thousand bright fancies and dreams at their
    core.

And its coralline clusters the mountain ash shakes,
Till they rattle in fiery hail to the ground ;
While the briar's red candles are lit in the brakes
Where the robin besprinkled with glory awakes,
Thrilling out his sweet soul to the echoes around.

And the honey-veined maple, beginning to flout
In the chill morning breath of the sudden winged blast,
Soon its deep-scarlet leaves shakes so ruthlessly out,
That like clouds of dead butterflies floating about,
They proclaim to the landscape that summer is past.

GOLD.

Prince of this sordid world, whose rayless throne,
From age to age has been the human heart,
Turning its kindliest feelings into stone,
Thou wak'st them only when thou wouldst impart
That guilty throb at which they seem to start
Forth in disinterested purity ;
Urging us, thy poor willing dupes, to feel
That heaven inspires the touch that sets them free,
'Till we at last, thou tenfold monster, kneel
On Deity itself to worship thee.

Religion's mantle, Friendship's beaming eyes,
The statesman, and the arbiter of fame,
The patriot, in his popular disguise,
The tongue of Eloquence, the titled name—
Offspring mayhap, of plunder, sword and flame—
The hero, too, whose sands in glory run,
All ! all ! to thy unconquered prowess yield—
They are the guilty trophies thou hast won—
The standing army of thy proudest field.

IMPROMPTU.

TWIN fountains sparkling side by side
Comingling their bright crimson spray,
And gushing in one glowing tide
Though hidden from the lignt of day,
  My darling, thus thy heart and mine.

And when in darksome pilgrim-hours
I wend my way through thorns to thee
I feel as though I tread on flowers
So dear the pathway is to me
  My only lamp, my saint, my shrine.

UNBORN.

There's something in my soul unsung!—
A flood of light behind a cloud,
A something that my struggling tongue
In vain essays to cry aloud!

But what it is or whence it flows
I can't divine, though, bright or dim,
It seems to be a fire that glows
Far down below the crater's brim.

And oft I think 'tis some great truth
Belonging to the higher spheres,
Whose mystic germs unknown to youth
Are planted in our later years.—

A secret struggling with the gloom
That it in vain attempts to brave—
A something that must burst and bloom
Beyond the portals of the grave.

"COME OUT FROM AMONG THEM."

"COME OUT FROM AMONG THEM."

Ho! Step out into broader light,
And shake thyself and lift thy head,
And backwards look into the night
       That thou hast fled.

Behold the revel and the rout,
And list the rattle of the box
That knocks the ivory souls about,
       With cunning knocks.

And mark the wanton's brow and cheek
Grow redder as each cup she drains
To him who has no power to break
       Her cursèd chains.

And count the madmen o'er and o'er,
That squander wealth and youth and time,
While huddled towards the gilded door
       That leads to crime.

And see them through the portal sweep,
Without one thought of being forgiven,
While stumbling down the awful steep
       That leads from heaven.

"*COME OUT FROM AMONG THEM.*"

Yes, stumbling farther from the skies,
Whiie ruin, at each footstep, starts
And paves the way with sunken eyes
          And broken hearts.

Though God should strike the daylight dead,
And make a desert of the sun,
'Twere brighter than the life they've led,
          Or what they've done.

Then step out into broader light,
And nerve thyself to smite the gloom,
'Till thou hast crushed the tenfold night
          Of such a doom.

THE ENCHANTRESS.

Thr table was rough, and a pine one;
The viands were coarse, sorry stuff,
And being scarcely sufficent to dine one,
The case it appeared hard enough,
"Till there laughingly sat down beside me
An enchantress whose magic untold
Spread the board with a feast, and supplied me
With luxuries dished up in gold.

GOLD.

I.

In the depths of a dim, sepulchral room
Where a pale, blue light seem'd to float in gloom,
And the wind, through the mouldering tapestry shreds,
Swung the spiders out the whole length of their threads,
Sat a frail old man in a worn-out vest,
With his gray eye fix'd on an iron chest;
He was cold without, and so cold within
That a palsy struck up a tune on his chin;
But, what cared he for being chill or old?
He grew young and warm near a fire of gold,
So his fleshless hand wandered o'er the lid
Till a spring revealed where the brands lay hid,
And he bent him low, with a quiv'ring gaze,
To play, all night, with their yellow blaze:
But, anon, he was seized with unearthly fear,
For a hollow voice chuckl'd into his ear :—

"Not a sous, old man, not a sous for the poor,
Let the orphan weep at your bolted door,
Let the famish'd dogs of the wint'ry blast
Lap the beggar's blood as he staggers past,
Hoard it up, old man, hoard it up with care,
Ha! ha!—what a glorious mine is there!"

Morning crept through the grating, bleak and chill,
But the eyes of the watcher were open still;
'Tho' so white his lips, and so fix'd his stare,
He now seem'd gazing in marble there!

II.

The dice box rattled, and the white balls flew,
And the wine-cup blazed with its gorgeous hue,
And the dark eye flashed with the fatal light
That the dog-star sheds on a sultry night,
When, a spirit, allured by the sinful glare,
Swooped along, unseen through the midnight air,
And join'd in the dance, with a step so fleet
That his huge, black plumes sung down to his feet;
While a frenzy swept through the festive hall
As he bowed and scraped to the queen of the ball,
And whispered a thought whose destruction stole
To the secret depths of her inmost soul.

And toyed with her lips and her dazzling cheek,
Till her young brain swam and her heart grew weak
And the tide of her passion came and fled
In unholy white and unholy red.
But, anon, in his awful mirth, he espied,
Scattering wealth untold upon every side,
The lord of the wassail, whose reckless hand
Fed with guilty gold all the crimes of the land;
Then, he paus'd and exclaimed, with a horrid leer,
"Ha! ha!—we shall soon have wild work here!"

Time still swept on, but the lights were fled,
The dance, long o'er, and the dancers dead,
Save a lone, old man who, in rags and tears,
Sung an idiot song of his early years!

III.

A mother caught the first tint of joy,
On the face of her half starv'd orphan boy,
As though his cheek were a poor, pale bud
Hanging over his young heart's crimson flood;
And as in ecstatic prayer she bent
O'er her loved one's breathing monument,

She wept when he feebly toss'd his head
And toyed, for once, with a crust of bread,—
Then, a spirit, down from the sunset steep,
Hung entranc'd o'er the pair as they sank to sleep,
While their trembling breath made his burning wings
Murmur low, like a thousand half-hush'd strings ;
When the flash of gold, from a youthful hand,
Swept his dyes, as it fell on the poor of the land
Dissolving the spell of the dull, cold ear
And the seal on the lips long voiceless here,
And the walls of the prisoned soul that lies
In the depths of the blind man's dungeon eyes :
Then, he shook from his plumes a deep presence out,
And soaring away, with a mighty shout
Exclaim'd, o'er the bright heaps thus laid bare,
"Oh ! God ! what a mine of bliss is there !"

The youth's fresh bloom had long pass'd away,
But his locks grew brighter every day,
'Till, at last, he was found one morn, 'tis said,
With an amber beam floating 'round his head !

INVOCATION.

INVOCATION.

Sing me a New-Year's song,
Let it be full of rhyme,
Like to the olden time
When, 'mid the bearded throng,
The flagons flashed along,
Till the blood began to climb
Up to the heated brows,
While all the festive boughs
Trembled in the glad chime
That rang out on the air,
From many a hoary spire,
While the gay peal grew higher,
Mid songs and laughter there.

Sing me a New-Year's song,
Let it be proud and strong
I want no sickly rhyme,
But a deep throated chime,

A shout from the olden time
Sonorous and sublime,
While beauty rules the feast,
And the flagon's crimson yeast,
Like rubies gleam upon the bearded chin.
As louder grows the din
'Till the brain begins to spin.
And the wassail runs to heavenly madness there,
And throws its red beams on the brave and fair.

LINES

Be still as the grave !—oh !—be still !
A young mother hugs her dead child,
With a look so appallingly wild,
That the only relief for such terrible grief
Is to let the poor thing hug her fill—
Be still as the grave !—oh !—be still !

'Tis the lioness of her despair
That howls 'mid the waste of her heart,
And tears every feeling apart;
'Till the pulse of her joys is as still as her boy's,
That's now coldly stiffening there—
'Tis the lioness of her despair.

Who'd pen up a torrent like this?
Darkly swollen with misery's snows,
The fount of her bosom o'erflows ;
While all we can trace in its waves, is that face
That now freezes the dew of her kiss—
Who'd pen up a torrent like this?

Yes,—now you may take her away—
That terrible hurricane's past,
And she too has sunk with the blast,
While her lips are as white as a glimpse of moonlight,
And her brow turns colder than clay—
Yes,——now you may take her away.

SPRING.

THE morning clouds are touched with mellow gold ;
   The scentless winds have ceased their angry strife ;
And, like Pygmalion's marble love of old,
   The frozen earth is warming into life.

The sullen air is melting into song ;
   The wayside sod is breaking into flowers ;
And merrily the streamlets dance along
   Through sunshine scattered amid shade and showers.

The bud upon the silver willow swells ;
   The crested grove is thickening in the skies,
Where the soft silken leaves, from out their shells,
   Peep like the early wings of dragon-flies.

The robin hymns the daylight down the west ;
   The giddy swallow twitters on the wing ;
And, like a sigh, warm from a maiden's breast,
   The gentle zephyr whispers " it is Spring."

"HOW LONG, O LORD?"

Mistaking for the clear, cool, sparkling rill
    The stagnant pool that skirts the sultry way,
The long-eared pilgrim blindly drinks his fill,
    And, turning round, anon begins to bray.

And thus it is with that dull tribe who think
    They slake their thirst at the Pierian spring;
They dip their muzzles in a steaming sink,
    Then, with distended jaws, begin to sing.

Oh, how shall we escape that triple curse—
    The plodding critic, publisher, and bard
Who leave true Genius with an empty purse,
    And make the way of Poesy so hard—

The publisher, with his Procrustean bed,
    Who cleverly permits a rusty nail
To pick the stubborn lock he calls "a head."
    While polished keys and cunning fingers fail—

The critic, too, who tramples down the rose,
    While tending the foul weeds that round it throng,
And breaks up in his lens of stupid prose
    The bright effulgence of immortal song—

And that dire enemy of tune and time,
    Who for ambrosia munches a dry crust,
And lies at last, a scavenger of rhyme,
    Beneath a monument of sweat and dust?

Oh, when shall heaven-born Genius take the field,
    And hurl this cruel triad from their throne,
And, Perseus-like, place on Minerva's shield
    The Gorgon head that turns them into stone?

COME!

Come shake out thy tresses, dark, dazzling and wild,
On the breath of the morn, like a beautiful child
That's at play with the winds on the flowery lea,
And haste my beloved one to me.

For thou art the spirit of sunshine and bloom,
That breathes all around me this subtle perfume,
And scatters the clouds and the tempests that roll
Through the innermost depths of my soul.

Oh! haste thee—Oh! haste, and give light to the day,
And perfume all the winds and the flowers on thy way;
With thy silvery voice wake the songs of the grove,
And breathe the one word that I love.

THE TENANT.

I ʙʀᴜsʜᴇᴅ away the thick and sombre dust of many
    years,
    And peeped in at the window of this pulseless heart
    of mine ;
But oh ! how soon I turned away in agonizing tears
    From such a gloomy sepulchre—from such a ruined
    shrine.

There, in the very centre of its one great vault sʜᴇ lay
    Stretched out upon the bier of all my withered joys
    and hopes,
The whiteness of her dead face being the only vivid ray
    That served to show how desolate those broken
    shafts and copes.

I whispered·" Oh ! my love !" but the pale rosebud
    opened not,

Nor flashed the slumbering violets from beneath their
 silken vail ;
Then I wildly clasped her to me, but no thrill electric
 shot
 Throughout her snowy bosom, or shook off her icy
 mail.

And I called her and beseeched her, till my frenzy shook
 the skies,
 And madly kissed her in the shadow of her raven
 hair ;
But she was cold to my embrace, and dead to all my
 cries,
 And lay as placidly as if she never knew me, there.

SPRING.

The spirits of air are beginning to rove
Among pathways that sparkle with sunshine and
    showers,
And to touch the chill depths of the hawthorn grove
Till they melt into music and burst into flowers.

And the skies are becoming as blue as a lake,
While the murmuring breezes, on tremulous plume,
Sing as low as a bee, in the eglantine brake
Where the primrose peeps out, like a star, through the
    gloom.

And the meadows are dancing through light and
    through shade ;
With a bright, balmy knot tossed in gold, here and there ;
While the heifer at eve that winds up through the glade,
With her mouth full of cowslips perfumes the whole air.

And the silvery voice of the crystaline brooks,
Echoes down through the dell with a magical tone,
Or is lost on the lea or in lone shaded nooks,
Among songs, sighs and whispers as sweet as its own.

THE OLDEN MELODY.

Sing on, sing on, for I remember well
Each strain of that sweet olden melody,
And if you mark a tear fall from my eye,
Sing on, sing on, 'tis only music's spell,
That 'wakes the memory of days gone by.

That song was ofttimes sweetly breathed to me,
By all I've ever loved or can love here,
And when its deep tones fell upon my ear,
They mellowed down my young heart's sunny glee,
To something that was sad, but O, 'twas dear.

Sing—thou canst sing me back to youth and bloom,
And should one fleeting moment mark my stay,
Think not it is too brief, for locks so gray,
Such gleams of sunshine cancel years of gloom,
E'en tho' they only flash and die away.

Why hast thou ceas'd?   I'm growing old again,
The stream plays colder round my listening heart,
Oh! dearest, dearest vision, must we part?
Would that some power now broke this mortal chain,
Then should I dwell with thee where e'er thou art.

NOON AND MIDNIGHT.

NOON !

ETERNAL ONE ! before thee now I stand,
And worship thee ; but not through these lost eyes,
Smitten to darkness by thy unseen Hand,
For purposes all wise.

To trace thy steps I need no outer ray,
For thou who dost these sightless orbs control,
Hast, in thy mercy, turned a tenfold day
In on my darkened soul.

Father, I see thee now, and the bright rays
That fall upon this tomb-like face of mine,
Are but as midnight to the inward blaze
Through which thy glories shine.

And, as I feel that the material sun
Might have estranged from thee, this erring mind,
Oh ! how I thank thee,—thou Eternal One—
That I am wholly blind !

MIDNIGHT !

OH ! what were life itself, if these bright eyes
Should close in darkness on this beauteous earth,
Where all my treasure—all my being lies,
And all my joys have birth?

How could I dwell locked up in hopeless night
Through which the faintest glimmer never stole,
And feel these eyes, once filled with living light,
The dungeon of my soul?

No stars, no skies, no fields, no vernal flowers
To glad, with one bright tint, or genial ray
The cold, bleak desert of Cimmerian hours,
Through which I grope my way

But gloom eternal, hanging o'er the path
That leads me shuddering from the joyous past.
Till some less cruel bolt of aimless wrath
Strikes out my life at last.

CHILD OF THE GOLDEN HAIR.

Child of the golden hair come, tell me now,
Where lies thy pathway through life's thorny wild?
On the unwritten page of that bright brow,
There's not a trace to tell me where, sweet child.

The clust'ring blossoms that thy feet surround,
The beam that now seems coiled about thy head,
Poor, early traveller, may, alas! be found
No index to the path that thou must tread.

There, in thy own young morning's sunny ray,
Regardless of the future and thy fate,
Thou'rt peeping merrily out upon the way,
Through the bright bars of youth's half open gate.

Thou can'st not dream—so innocent thou art—
'That that young breast may be an, unheaved sigh,
Or that there's now shut down on thy young heart,
The dim, dark, floodgates of a wanderer's eye.

Child of the golden hair, remember this,—
Wherever gloom falls o'er that path of thine,
There thou may'st find some gems of hidden bliss.
For, child, thou art the miner and the mine.

Remember, should'st thou plume thy wings for flight.
The sounding pinions never need be furl'd
'Till thou hast reach'd that Himalayan height
That looks sublimely down upon the world.

THE SPECTRE.

WHEN the path is lone and the tempest 's high,
And the beggar's lamp 's blown out in the sky ;
When with upturned face neither near nor far
Can he catch a glimpse of one rushlight star ;
When he feebly tucks round his withered breast
All that now remains of his threadbare vest,
And turns in the blast, ere he sink in death,
To cough, and gasp for a moment's breath,
While the tattered flag of his thin, white hair
Wildly floats o'er the staff that he leans on there,
Then, Angel of Pity, steal behind,
With your wing spread between him and the wind !

NIGHT.

When on dim pinions the departing day
Droops, like an angel dying in the West,
With the red glory smitten on his breast,
Till the last trembling beam has pass'd away,

Then, dost thou mount thy glitt'ring throne, oh ! Night !
And grasp thy shining ball—the orbéd moon ;
Waxing in regal splendor, till thy noon
Is one soft blaze, thou ethiop queen of light.

The moon !—What gorgeous robes of state are thine—
The jewell'd ether o'er thy shoulders flung,
And burning vesper on thy forehead hung,
While countless gems thy raven locks entwine.

And, then, the palace halls thou tread'st below—
Dell, wood and glade be-pearl'd with dewy showers,
As though the heavens were toss'd from airy towers
In silvery shot, when melted in thy glow.

Dell, wood and glade—thy votaries' hush'd retreat
When flowery carpets, from the green sward spun
By the long, golden fingers of the sun,
Sparkle and blush beneath their dripping feet.

Thy votaries—Ah, but who shall tell of these—
Of quiv'ring soul and lip, and flashing cheek
As if the very life-blood rush'd to speak
When the tongue swooned in blissful agonies.

Yes,—welded lip to lip in love's hot blast
And souls that strike the eyes into a blaze,
And flood their crystal chambers with such rays,
That blind with ecstasy they fail at last.

Enchantress,—these are thine, and thine alone—
The bright, the beautiful, love's holy trance—
All win a rapture from thy dreamy glance,
To the broad, soulless glare of day unknown.

SONG OF THE SALE.

WELL booted and spur'd for a trip,
  A bailiff rode forth in the storm,
Sunk in furs and in pilot cloth up to his lip,
And his costly cap slouched with a satisfied dip
While his huge over-alls, buttoned up to his hip,
  Kept his stout legs cosy and warm.

  His horse, plump and black as a sloe,
  Shook his shining mane out on the gale ;
And with nostrils, like patches of flame, all a-glow,
Bore him gallantly on through the pitiless snow,
At a pace far from poverty-stricken, I trow,
  As he sung the song of the sale :—

  "Going !—going ! !—gone ! ! !
  The bed and the bedstead and all,
Even down to the chair the poor widow sits on,
In her clean, scanty raiment that once was the ton,
With her sweet, marble face, lonely, tearful and wan,
And her heavy eyes fixed on the wall.

"The turf, like the bed, must be sold—
　Let the fire be pitched out in the snow—
Though the mother and little ones perish with cold,
The respectable absentee must have his gold ;
For he gambles and drinks and gives dinners untold,
　Like " a jolly, good fellow," we know.

"What, though she falls down in a swoon,
　With a cry of the wildest despair,
When she sees the lov'd cradle and tea-cup and spoon
That belonged to her angel—God's last, frailest boon,—
Who had passed like a bud that had opened too soon.
　Knocked down to some purchaser there ?

"And what recks it to me or to you,
　If the scoundrel 's the vilest of men ;
Should he fail to the tune of a thousand or two,
When he rings from his victim the very last " sous "
He'll quickly get " white-washed," till spick and span
　new,
　He begins operations again ?

SONG OF THE SALE.

"Then dose them, I say, with the laws,
 Till their long, empty gullets are crammed;
For the wealthy have always an excellent cause,
And need never be hanging their beggarly jaws,
Or be craving forever with bottomless maws;
 So, the poor and the needy, be damned!"

THE SIX HUNDRED.

"Take the guns, Nolan said."—Tennyson.

Take the guns, Nolan said—On dashed the light Brigade !
Look to it England, and look at it France ;
Through the fierce havoc of shot, shell and shining blade,
Six hundred horsemen now boldly advance.
Six hundred brave fellows hard holding their breath—
Six hundred that ride like a hunt, into death !
As they rush from the hill, take them in at a glance,
And mark every man while his gallant heart burns.
Oh ! count the Six Hundred !—Count, England ! Count,
      France !
And count him a million, that ever returns !

Look, down through the glen !—through the curst fiery
   glen !
Look, England, as from the deep gorges they sally,
The Russians are pelting your six hundred men,
With dark, iron lightning along the whole valley !
Six hundred to cope with so mighty a host !
Six hundred—a handful—they all must be lost !
Help, England !—They don't get a moment to rally,
Though each of them throws up a breast-work of dead ;
Why stand you there keeping the terrrible tally ?
There's no help in the ashes you strew on your head.

Oh ! can it be wondered.—Oh ! can it be wondered,
When England and France must look on in dismay,
None can help them or sunder them ?—They can't be
   sundered !
Though their sabres and lances are melting away.
Though they're fighting, a hundred !—a thousand to one !
They have killed every gunner that stood by his gun,
But they can't take the guns in so wild an affray—
The wildest affray that has ever yet thundered !
But England can sob out through all her dismay :—
If Greece has her Three—I have got my Six. Hun-
   dred !

'Turn away from the glen—from the dark fatal glen !
And tell you can't witness so murderous a stroke ;
For the doomed Light Brigade's riding back once again,
But a few wounded men, grim with blood and with
    smoke !—
But a few mangled heroes that still cannot live,
Till they've ridden, once more, through a shot and
    shell sieve.
Oh! England, they've come !—though with anguish
    you choke,
Run and kiss them, and grasp where their hands ought
    to be ;
And bear up, if you can, for though fearful the stroke,
It has won a Thermopylæ, glorious to thee !

NATIONAL MUSIC.

In mansions built of the mouldering bones
Of those who died from the want of bread,
The great of the land, blend their happy tones
As their festal halls they gayly tread.

Grim skulls are the lamps that hang around ;
Their oil is the widow's silent tear ;
And the dust of the orphan strews the ground
That's made from the houseless stranger's bier.

While the cup's red draught, from the heart is trod.
A nation's sighs dim the jewel's blaze,
That hangs on the breast of some noble clod
Who reels through the dance's giddy maze.

But, is not the music sad and wild ?
It falls on the ear like a dying shriek ;
The ALTO's sung by a hungry child,
With a scalding drop on his pallid cheek.

And the Treble's sobb'd by the decent poor
Who tried to conceal their hapless fate,
'Till the Landlord drove them to the door,
And bared to the world, their wretched state.

And the Tenor's raved in a mother's pray'r,
As she wildly clings to her starving boy,
While angels weep o'er the ragged pair
Who had never tasted a moment's joy.

And the Bass is an old man's feeble groan,
Who toils here below with sighs and tears,
For a piece of a coarse brown loaf, alone,
Though bow'd with the weight of three-score years.

And the Chorus bursts in wild despair,
From the bloodless lips of a countless throng,
While a heart-string breaking here and there,
Beats sullen time, to the mournful song.

But the dancers still move gayly by ;
Or turn to the helpless, famish'd band,
To ask who it is, that dares to sigh
When he sings for the great of a Christian land.

THE FORBIDDEN PATH.

Nor across that field of clover !
  Not across that field I say ;
Don't you see my eyes run over ?
  I must go another way.

Child. its very balm would kill me ;
  And the path I used to tread
Would, through all its windings, fill me
  With the presence of the dead.

Though I'm always looking at her
  With the far-light on her brow,
In her beauty,—but, no matter ;
  Do not bring her nearer now.

For I could not bear the gladness
  That would then around me beam ;
As I should but wake to madness,
  When I found it but a dream.

IMPROMPTU ON A BEAUTIFUL BUTTERFLY.

FRAILEST of all earth's lovely things,
Uncertain wanderer that swings
Upon those gaudy, rose-leaf wings
    In yonder sky,
What of the blight that Autumn brings
    To thee by and bye?

Half-helpless in the summer air,
The sport of wanton breezes there,
How, thoughtless creature, shalt thou bear
    The ruthless blast
That, with the chill of time and care,
    Strikes thee at last ?

Flushed gossamer, thou hast thy day—
Thy morn and noon of sunny play ;
And, sportive creature, tell me, pray,
    What more have we ?
We flutter, too, and pass away,
    Bright thing, like thee.

LINES.

If thou would'st search the earth, from pole to pole,
For deepest knowledge of the human soul,
With steady hand the balance you must hold,
And weigh with miser eye the dross and gold.
That keen perception, that gigantic mind
That opes alone, " the volume of mankind,"
Each seeming worthless tittle stoops to scan,
'Tis oft the faithful index to the man.
Mark,—he who would deny his inward lot,
Must struggle to appear what he is not,
And some weak effort will in time reveal,
The very thing, 'twas hoped it would conceal.
No soul on earth, howe'er disguised it be,
But in some trait, shows its epitome,
There still remains a vulnerable part,
A vista teeming with the naked heart,
E'en famish'd nature bursts her icy chain
Where Arctic snows, hold their eternal reign,
To own a germ within her bosom lies,
That would have bloomed beneath some other skies.

A HERO OF A HUNDRED FIGHTS.

On a rich couch, where costly tissues fall
From curious bars, in many a gorgeous fold
Lit up with gleaming threads of tinted gold,
In splendid mockery of his funeral pall,
And sweeping the bright dyes of ancient Tyre
That seem to blaze upon the marble floor,
Lies a famed Chief—his vaunted victories o'er—
Who revelled life away in blood and fire,
But feels—alas too late—war's hellish pulse no more.

Watching the fearful tellings of his eye,
In anxious whispering groups around him stand
Warrior and prince—the magnates of the land,
Waiting to see the aged hero die,
Who closed and grappled hand and hand with death,

So oft, on many a glorious battle field,
Ere he would one of those bright laurels yield ;
And thus, regardless of his mortal breath,
Laughed when the gloomy tyrants thunders round him
      pealed.

He heeds them not,—his heart is with the past,
Struggling to free itself from seas of gore,
Whose clotted waves roll over it, on ? more.—
The day of retribution's come at last,
In answer to the widow's wild "Amen !"
And drags him on from reeking plain to plain,
Amid the spectre armies of his brain,
To fight his country's battles o'er again
And purge its paltry honor from some fancied stain.

The past and future are the dungeon walls
That close upon his shuddering spirit now,
And set their rayless seal upon his brow
That turns from every earthly thing, and palls :
For all those crimson dyes seem tinged with blood,
And the gold threads gleam out like battle fires,
While the rich perfume that the East expires
Steals o'er their bones, who once beside him stood,
And fell, as bravely fell their noble hearted sires !

Death loads him down with chains, securely press'd.—
His clammy arm deals its last dreamy blow ;
And yielding up its sword to the grim foe,
Falls shivering down upon his laboring breast.
His heartstrings burst with a convulsive groan—
To the poor weeping herd, a peaceful sigh !—
And prince and warrior transported fly
To turn him into monumental stone,
And add to their great stock another marble lie.

THE STORM STAR.

The heavens with sudden clouds and rain
Were dark and dismal as the tomb ;
Though sometimes, in a feeble stain,
The moon oozed through the deepening gloom ;
The thunders, too, began to boom
And swing their sledges swift and high ;
And swing them swifter, swing them higher,
And smash the gates that shut the sky,
And dash them down in bars of fire.

The storms—the mighty storms were out,
Tumbling the hills into the dales,
And knocking the great sea about
Far up the heavens in smoky gales ;
And angry rivers swept the vales ;
And forests crashed and castles fell ;
And rocks came tumbling everywhere,
And hamlet roofs, from out the dell,
Like scattered rooks, swept through the air.

'Twas at this hour, and in a cave
That seemed some monster gaping wide,
As if about to gulp the wave
That leaped from out the maddening tide,
And foaming lashed its rocky hide,
Between its savage jaws there stood,
'Mid rows of huge stalactite teeth,
A figure drenched with fire or blood
That streamed out o'er the gorge beneath.

For fire and blood it glowed, in turn;
But still 'twas fire—fierce, flameless fire,
Where huge flamingoes seemed to burn
And not the driftwood mounting higher
On that mysterious midnight pyre,
Till all around, above, below,
On which the lurid radiance fell,
Seemed bathed in that appalling glow
That reddens in the mouth of hell

Spar upon spar the specter threw
In frantic haste upon the pile,
Till off to sea the signal flew,
A crimson star, for many a mile;

Yet meant, perchance, but to beguile
Some storm-tossed sail on such a night,
To struggle through the breaker's roar,
Still hoping in that faithless light,
Till dashed in fragments on the shore.

But gaze upon that manly form—
That noble face and lofty brow,
And say if he would aid the storm
In all that it is working now,
Or lure some helpless, hapless prow,
Till on that wild and stormy beach
Her shattered bales and gold lay spread,
Till he—accursèd one—could reach
And snatch them from among the dead.

But no ! that fire is but a spark
Of one that all his soul consumes ;
And meant to guide one struggling bark
That now, he fears the tempest dooms ;
For as the ocean louder booms,
He shakes with anguish and affright ;
And feels in all his dire dismay,
It can not live through such a night,
Or round into the sullen bay.

That bark, if now 'twere on the deep,
Had left at eve the Fisher's Isle,
When winds and waves were both asleep,
Beneath the early moonbeam's smile.
And one fair being bore, the while——
The Fisher-maiden of his love,
Who ofttimes stole to meet him there ;
He knew she'd see the shining dove,
And knew, alas ! what she would dare.

Nor should that beacon fire have burned,
Had not the winds been lulled to rest,
After the crimson sun was urned
Within one dark cloud in the west—
One cloud that reared its awful crest
And suddenly seized on the sky,
And blotted out the world below,
And bade the red-winged lightnings fly,
And bade the dark-winged tempest blow.

But now, too late to quench that flame,
For it had burned an hour or more
Ere down the storm and darkness came
To sweep away that lonely shore,
So thus he seeks its beams of gore

To throw out broader on the sea,
That they may touch her failing boat,
If on that wild immensity
Perchance it yet should keep afloat.

Oh! dread and horrible retreat!—
The green-backed billows, finned with foam,
Now rush up to his very feet,
And almost make the cave their own,
Shaking with thunder its red dome,
While spars and masts come drifting in,
And rest upon the shelving rock,
Until his brain begins to spin
And sink beneath the deadly shock.

Another wave, more huge and dark,
Now rolls in on the rocky floor;
But, heavens! it bears a tiny bark
Still bending to a tiny oar!
Till now within the cavern door,
A dripping maiden towards him sweeps
In all her pale, dishevelled charms,
And forward with a low cry leaps,
And fainting, falls into his arms!

TO AN EMBALMED HUMMING BIRD.

Why look so sad ? The sunbeam 'round thee flings
The mellow light through which thou once didst stray,
Arouse thee, sleeper ! shake thy golden wings;
Thy pathway lies along its glittering ray ;
This is thy own, thy native evening hour,
Why tarry, traveller of the closing flower?

Ah, thou wilt sport no more, when twilight's near,
Through all those glories that soon fade in night ;
Nor dews begem thee o'er, 'till thou appear
A flying fragment of embodied light;
Nor balmy zephyrs ever bear along,
The hum that was their dazzling playmate's song.

The restless moments that still o'er thee sweep,
Still spare thee in this endless deep repose,
For here thou art, as if thou wert asleep,
Upon the bosom of the moonlit rose ;
The rainbow hue still on thy plumage lingers,
Unsullied by decay's dim, dusty fingers.

But, something, though in all this splendor drest,
To chase that pensive gloom is wanting still.
A heart to throb within that tiny breast,
A busy eye that speck of void to fill ;
For oh ! 'tis sad to see such beauty wear
That silent, moveless, melancholy air.

The artist's hand may war with thee, O, death !
And gild thy terrors, but how vain the strife
Till he can conjure back the fleeting breath,
And 'rouse again the slumbering pulse of life,
Light up the eye, and learn the mystic art
That sends the life-blood flashing through the heart.

THE PRIMROSE.

The first pale primrose, like a fallen star,
Unheeded lay within a grassy dell,
Till bright Aurora from her beaming car,
Threw o'er the dewy gem her golden spell.

By chance, a maiden slumb'ring in the vale,
With balmy lips unconscious touched it then,
And on it poured so exquisite a gale,
The fragrance never left its leaves again.

And thus, 'tis whispered, from that very hour,
Whene'er the woodland blossoms fade in death,
The hue and odor of this gentle flower
Return to sunshine and a maiden's breath.

BURIED FLOWERS.

In that brown husk that by the wayside lies,
  The sport of biting winds and bitter showers,
Are folded up a thousand beamless dyes
  That yet shall flash amid the realm of flowers.

And ofttimes thus, from lessening day to day,
  We meet, while traveling onward to the tomb,
Some poor, lone, human husk upon the way,
  That's filled, to bursting, with eternal bloom.

CLOUDS.

Sweet hollows in the ripple of God's smile,
Where His deep alchemy forever dwells,
Mapping out all that's beautiful, the while,
In soft delicious dews, and showery spells
That lie in silver on the heather bells
That spread, like plum-bloom, o'er the mountain height,
And sky it over with dim, purple light.
How often in the sultry summer hours,
Has languid Nature crept beneath your tent
So cool and lovingly above her bent,
"Till, in a sunny dance of crystal showers,
The aërial canopy was gayly rent,
And downwards on her grateful breast was poured
The balm that all her energies restored.

"MISS NIGHTINGALE."

UNDER FANCIFUL TREATMENT. *

WHERE the waves of the Euxine but bend a mere stream,
 Miss Nightingale sits by them all the night long;
And the poor wounded soldier oft thinks it a dream,
 As she tends him and lulls him to sleep with her song,

The soft touch of her hand he can never forget;
 But oft when at home at the close of the year,
He'll think that Miss Nightingale sings for him yet,
 And before her bright image, in dreams, bend him
  here.

Mid the heroes that perished beside that dark wave,
 What thousands were rescued while yet their eyes
  shone;
For a balm was distilled from her presence, that gave
 A fresh tint to their cheek, when it's color was gone.

And the sailor and soldier, till memory dies,
 Shall breath of that vision through every year;
And, as bright to his soul as she was to his eyes,
 At the sound of her sanctified name bend him here.

* Verb. Sap.

UP IN THE MORN.

Through the woods!   Through the woods!   Up in the
    morn,
To the bay of the hound, and the clang of the horn
Come, 'rouse thee and slip from the leash the loud pack
Till they burst in full cry on the deer's subtle track.

No delicate pallor shall spread o'er thy face,
But the manly—the berry-brown tinge of the chase ;
For the tint of thy cheek, and the light of thine eye,
Shall be caught from the winds, and be caught from
    the sky.

Far over the mountains, and down through the vales,
Where the rivers are rippled by shallows and gales,
And the crimson-flecked trout in the shining waves lie,
"Till betrayed from their depths by the false, fatal fly.

There, there shalt thou roam at the first peep of dawn,
With the strength of a lion and step of a fawn ;
And the smooth, silken line swiftly spin from the reel,
When the shining prey's struck with that fly's sting of
    steel.

Through the woods ! Through the vales !—Up in the
    morn,
When the daybreak of purple-edged sunbeams is born
When the earth flashes forth its first emerald hue,
In a myriad bright beams that are prismed in dew.

Then shall beauty, and vigor, and pleasure be thine,
With a lightness of heart that is almost divine ;
And thy life's happy history be that of a sage,
With a sunbeam to fall on its very last page.

THE KERRY GIRL.

SMILING brightly till her teeth of pearl
   Burst the dewy rose-bud of her lips,
See how yonder blooming Kerry girl
   O'er the crystal streamlet gayly trips.

Hark, how loudly now her laugh is ringing,
   While her bounding steps become more fleet ;
Till, at last, half startled she is flinging
   Showers of liquid diamonds from her feet.

Softly now the flowery bank she presses,
   With her lovely features in a blaze,
For the snood that bound her raven tresses,
   Has let them fall in one bewitching maze.

But quickly o'er the sparkling mirrored waters,
  Rippling in their beauty through the glen,
See her bend like one of Eve's own daughters,
  . Binding the bright treasure up again.

Oh, parting sunbeams, from the brooklet, never
  Let this wondrous vision disappear ;
But frame it in these silvery waves forever,
  And I will live and die a pilgrim here.

FISHERMAN'S SONG.

WHEN morning builds a jewelled heap
  Of sands and sea-shells on the shore,
We brothers of the purple deep,
Aroused from sleep,
  Bend to the silver-dripping oar.

And to our joyous matin song
  That echoes answer far and wide,
A living and a shadowed throng
We sweep along,
  In double glory o'er the tide,

Till gathering up each netted fold
  In which our shining treasure lies,
We seem to draw from depths untold
A web of gold,
  Shot with a thousand brilliant dyes.

And thus while glide the hours away,
   We gayly heap the sunny spoils
That flashed throughout the livelong day,
As though there lay
   A tangled rainbow in our toils.

Till buried in his crimson urn,
   The sun proclaims our labors o'er,
And joyously our eyes we turn
To those that burn
   Beside our far-off cottage door.

LIFE'S TURNPIKE GATE.

I've travelled down this weary, broken track—
    This heartless vista swept by the lone wind—
And here I pause a moment to look back
    On all the windows that lie quenched behind ;
And gazing thus, I weeping seek in vain
My early frost-work on one single pane.

Alas ! the music of each turnpike gate—
    That once so joyously swung out my years—
With jarring hinge, too soon began to grate
    On every nerve, and on those once glad ears,
And grate so harshly that no other sound
Now 's heard between its opening and rebound.

When shall the last ope on my tottering way—
    That way of blighted buds and darkened flowers?
My eyes have long been groping for the day,
    Or inward gazing on those happy hours
'Mid which SHE stood !—the angel of my soul—
And brightened, with her life and love, the whole !

But, hark !—what sounds !—and what celestial light !
  The last gate !—rolling back with golden bars !
And see !—what bursts upon my new-born sight !
  An angel !—waiting there, hung round with stars !
The hinge once more pours forth his harmony !
The angel joins !—Oh ! heavens ! tis she ! tis she !

THE CONVOLVULUS.

Bright and beautiful star of the day-break of flowers,
How serenely thy glory steals forth while we sleep;—
And how oft, from the tint of the first purple hours,—
Do we fancy their beams from thy dewy bell creep.

But at noon, when we seek for that exquisite glow,
All thy delicate petals are then folded up;
But we break not the spell by a touch, for we know
That some spirit of dawn lies concealed in the cup.

TURKISH MAIDEN'S SONG.

On the wild, shaded banks of the Tamour there grew
A young lily whose cup was o'erflowing with dew,
When a bulbul once stole, after sunset, and drained
The pure chalice of all the bright drops it contained.

And the beautiful flower that so often was chilled
By the glittering flood that its bosom had filled,
Felt an exquisite pang when the wing of the bird
Through its tremulous leaves like a summer wind
    stirred.

And each evening the reveller afterwards came,
When he found the cup full and th nectar the same,
And still drank of its depths from a sheltering thorn,
Singing over his bright little goblet till morn.

But the lily that once by the Tamyris grew,
And the bulbul that drank from its chalice of dew,
Now no more by those bright glancing waters love
    on ;—
The chalice is broken !—the bulbul is gone !

LINES

WRITTEN AT PETERBOROUGH, CANADA, APRIL, 1859.

Has the frost that Time cunningly strews through my
    hair,
Or the shadow that Age seeks to throw o'er my eye,
Made these scenes of my youth seem less happy and fair
Than they looked in the days now forever gone by ?

There's no solitude here ! All is bustle and strife
In pursuit of that weary philosopher's stone ;
And my old shaded haunts pant with clamorous life,
Though they once moved to song and soft whispers
    alone.

Give me back the " pine bushes," so changeles   in
    bloom,
Where the robin sang loud to his sober-hued love,
And the sweet-scented resin breathed forth its perfume
Till I fancied huge censers were swung through the
    grove.

Though the voice of the river is heard by me still,
Yet it seems but to moan a sad tale in my ear,
And I think 'tis a death-watch that ticks in the mill,
For the quick, joyous clack that once came out so clear.

But the bitter tears turn this pale cheek to a rill,
As I haste from one spot that I cannot endure,
Near the crumbling log school-house and church on the
     hill,
Where I oftentimes knelt when my heart was more
     pure ;

When the stars that beamed down through that once
     joyous tide
Lit it up with a grateful and rapturous glow :
But alas ! where they now through its cold waters glide
To be quenched in the darkness that's lurking below.

All is changed ! E'en the leaves seem but trembling to
     fall
While the bird's mellow song sounds complainingly
     sweet,
But the saddest—the most agonizing of all,
Is the throng of strange faces I pass in the street !

TRUTH.

With the thews of an angry lion strung
On a mammoth's bones that the earth staggers under ;
With an Ætna for each laboring lung,
And a voice that out-thunders tenfold thunder ;

With an eye in whose blaze the sun might die,
And a brow striking mortals dumb with terror,
And a foot like a mountain, poised on high
Oe'r the neck of the sovereign monster, Error,—

Thus I'll stalk through the midst of your mighty kings,
While their joints and their regal bawbles rattle,
And roar out the list of accursèd things
They have done to their herds of human cattle.

And I'll tell to the sordid scepter'd cheats,
With their blood-stain'd hands and their hoards of plunder,
They may yet be dragg'd through the common streets,
By the slaves they so long have trodden under.

And I'll tell of the great and the rich and the proud
In their costly robes upon eider sleeping,
While the poor man lies in the ragged shroud
That's to wrap his corse when he's not worth keeping.

And I'll tell of the gorgeous web they wear,
That its crimson woof and its warp of pearl
Are but gilded strings that the masters tear
From the broken heart of the Factory girl.

And I'll tell of the mine and the lives that pass
Down where time never spreads a sunlit pinion,
But the weary coal dust sinks in his glass,
Till they all are swept from its dark dominion.

But what shall I tell of the sterling man,
Whether peasant or prince, who is true to his brother,
Who cheerfully do's all the good that he can,
With a heart that unconscious'y feels for another?

To him, with a seraph's tongue, I'll say,
Push bravely on in the way you're going,
Till your locks are bright with a glorious gray,
And your measure of life is overflowing,

And when, at the close of your proud career,
You are just on the verge of the grave reclining,
You'll find yourself robed for a happier sphere,
With a passport that needs no countersigning.

NECTAR !

I'LL not bathe in the deep, red gulf of the cup,
  Where billows of sunset roll,
And the sparkling diamonds that bubble up,
  Break in foam on the burning soul.

I'll not dive far down through the mantling flood
  Till I reach the silvery plain,
While the ruby rapture blends with my blood
  And flashes in fire to my brain.

But a nectar far more divine I'll sip
  Than that which I'd quaff beneath,
From a cup whose brim is a rosy lip,
  And whose foam is pearly teeth :

Where the wine that entrances all my powers,
  Till I, trembling, no more can bear,
Is the dew that nursed by those gems and flowers,
  Lies in liquid sunbeams there.

HUMOROUS POEMS.

THE RAPE OF THALIA.

Half the gods and Saint Patrick were "off for the day,"
  And the wit and the wine had begun to run high,
When they suddenly heard, with a look of dismay,
  From the heights of Olympus old Jupiter cry:

"Ho! to arms!   Horse and foot!   Man the walls!
    Close the gates!
  Seize the Muses, whatever the jades are about,
And stick them in limbo, despite of the Fates,
  For there's treason among them, and I'll stamp it
    out!"

It now became certain, from all that was known,
  That what caused the red clouds and so fearful a
    racket,
Was a charge just preferred, at the foot of the throne,
  By three glorious Celestials, Payne, Forrest, and
    Hackett.

IMAGE EVALUATION
TEST TARGET (MT-3)

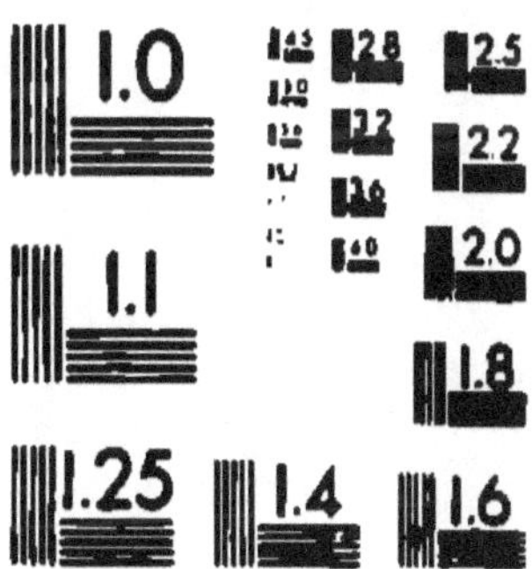

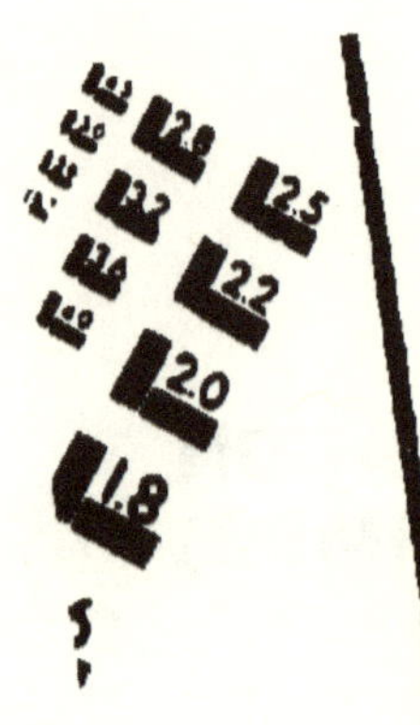

It set forth that Thalia had wantonly dared
   To treat them as if they were natives of Zama,
Having turned up her nose and quite coolly declared,
   That she would not inspire the "American drama."

When Jupiter read it, he—trembling with ire—
   Snapt his teeth, just as if they belonged to a beagle,
And exclaimed, "What! the hussy! refuse to inspire
   The people to whom I have lent my best eagle!"

"Ho, out there!   Let Tantalus have some salt cod!
   I'll punish all rebels; that you may rely on,
Let Sisyphus carry that stone in a hod!
   And let somebody rock-oil the wheel of Ixion.

But the word from Olympus had come down too late;
   For an old warder's wife said her husband had told
     her
That a few nights before, there slipped out of his gate
   A strange wight with a long, lively bag on his shoul-
     der!

When this became known it increased the uproar,
   And multitudes after the kidnapper sped ;
But soon all, save Hermes, came back once more,
   With a *non est inventus !* and shake of the head.

But he, like the rest, now returned home again,
   Sad and musing at each weary step that he took,
'Till before the dread "father of gods and of men"
   He appeared with a terribly woe-begone look !

"Have you got her?" said Jupiter, still all on fire,
   "Or the blackguard that carried her off in the sack?"
"I have seen her !" said Hermes, "have seen her, dread
     sire !
   But, alas ! she refuses, point blank, to come back."

"And where?" cried his majesty, looking quite wild,
   "Tell me, where? 'till I pelt them with lightning
     and thunder !
Speak ! you vagabond : speak ! Don't you know she's
     my child?
   No time must be lost ! We must tear them asunder."

"Sire, I've travelled," said Hermes, "both faithful and
    fast,
And have sought my half-sister from Pekin to Cork,
And where do you think that I found her at last?
    With a fellow called Fogarty, down in New York;"

"Ho! saddle a thunderbolt, Mercury, I say!
    'Tis swifter than winged cap or sandal, and tougher,
And seek for Thalia, and bear her this way,
    And if she cuts up any didos, handcuff her."

Now when Jupiter nods, gods, in squads, bound whole
    rods,
    And so Hermes flew off with some ten or eleven;
But ere noon he came back, not so spry, by long odds,
    For Thalia was not to be coaxed back to heaven!

And, besides, those who should have reported the case,
    Her eight loving sisters, declared, with a scoff,
That they scarcely could tell when they last saw her
    face,
    Though, just now, they believed some one carried
    her off!

It was now that the shout and fierce light filled the sky,
  Which the rev'lers, though treading their roseate
    mazes,
Knew was Jupiter's voice, and the glare of his eye,
  And that something had set the "old man" mad as
    blazes !

So they all in an instant sprang clean to their feet—
  Save Saint Patrick, who just had replenished his
    cup—
And taking a funny bee-line to the street,
  They, at once, in amazement, found out what was up.

Soon the warders were perched on the outermost walls
  Among blue-winged police that were ripe for a job ;
While the frightened Hesperides fled from their stalls,
  And left all their apples a prey to the mob !

Doors were bolted, and shutters were quickly put up,
  While **some**, who had heard not the summons aright,
Being aware that Saint Patrick was "taking a sup,"
  Just believed it was "only a bit of a fight."

Now, when Jupiter heard what was said by his son,
  He sprang into the air forty feet off his throne;
And forgetting his daughter and all she had done,
  Gave himself up to one consternation alone.

With a terrible roar and a stride of ten yards,
  "What?" he cried, while the skies with his light-
      nings were riven;
"Down to Tartarus sweep all the warders and guards!
  What, in thunder!—an Irishman let into heaven!"

NOT "MAL-DE-MER!"

On his recent homeward voyage from England, Dr. Oliver Wendell Holmes, the famous *littérateur* and scientist, suffered severely from *mal-de-mer*, or sea-sickness.—*Morning Paper.*

GREETING.

COME, clever, quaint and curious Master Bull,
    You owe us one !—Look to your laurels, sir !
We're cunning dogs, and must be paid in full,
    Send us a Roland for our Oliver !

The keel that our Promethean envoy bore
    To your fair land across the western main,
Has run an "ocean lane" from shore to shore
    That never, never should be closed again.

Let not your champion falter if he hears
    That our tough customer, who had been met
On the *Atlantic, Monthly*—aye, for years—
    Was, at long last, by *mal-de-mer* upset.

'Tis false !   The angry ocean's wildest swoop
    Had failed to stretch him on his cabin floor ;
He never lost his temper, legs, or soup ;
    He was a little Holmes sick—nothing more !

KITTY CLARE.

Wins those dark eighteen-pounders of yours, Kitty Clare--
So relintlessly blazin' away at me there--
Melt in rapturous tears to the low gushin' tone
Of your first lullaby, whin you're saited alone
Wid a bright little downy-cheeked sthranger that tipples,
Wid his soft rosy lips, at your sthrawberry nipples,
All so smothered in crame of their own for his sake,
Blur alive ! what a bewtiful piether you'll make !

And, besides, you can tache him so nate, your own way ;
From your hair and your eyes he can larn night and day,
And find roses and pearls in your teeth and your lips,
And the purest of snow at the fountain he sips.
While its music's own self he'll be larnin, galore,
Whin he hears that sweet voice of yours, Kitty asthore :
And whine'er you lane o'er him, asleep or awake,
Blur alive ! what a bewtiful piether you'll make !

IMPROMPTU.

On Mario, the celebrated singer declaring his intention of going to the Crimea, to fight under the banner of Victor Emmanuel, King of Sardinia.

What, now?—Signor Tenore, what's the matter?
You, whom we used to fête and feed and flatter,
Now going to rob us of our purest pleasures ;
You, who have been so long our ears delighting
    With your Andante and Allegro measures,
And gambols through the much astonished gamut,
Come, tell us, have you lost your senses—damn it !
    It's some new piece we want and not your fighting.

In spite of France, Victoria or Emmanuel,
Or all the rest, the Russ, may chance to tan you well.
A rolling fire is not your proper rôle :
Your troupe, Signor, should never be at war,
  Nor be a troop of horse ; and, 'pon my soul,
Our Cantatrices sha'n't be Cantinières,
Or if in love with military airs,
    They shall not take them from "Etoile du Nord,"

And, then, suppose, for instance, that a bullet
Should even graze your thorax or your gullet,
You might, forever afterwards, be wheezy ;
And when Sardinia was to peace restored,
   And you unto the arms of Giulia Grisi,
I can assure you, you'd look very droll,
With all your honors at your button hole,
   To find " *come gentil*" was not encored.

Or when you met the " Rounds " at night, I'll wager
If " who goes there?" was sung out, in G major,
You'd lose yourself, and quite forget the word ;
And if there followed, " stranger, quickly tell,"
You'd answer, in a fine sonorous third,
With such a glorious run and mellow roar
As fine, old Braham gave in days of yore,
" Above, be-e-e-low, good-night, all's well."

Although her faith to you may never waver,
This crotchet must make Donna Giulia quaver—
To see you madly rushing into Russia,
Where all the armies of the mighty Czar—
Or some of them, at least,—are sure to crush you :
And just because, you who have shone so long
In one bright sphere, the Lucifer of song,
Should fancy to become a shooting star.

Stay where the tenor of your way is blest ;
The Opera suits your operations best,
What do you care for a small country King ?
You who have robbed the critics of their spleen ;
You who have made the pit and boxes ring ;
The Crimea you would find in such a state,
That you'd cry *mea culpa*, when too late,
Like that old, titled noodle, Aberdeen.

SERENADE.

Au ! thin, come to the windy, my own Peggy Gorman ;
  'Though it's late, sure you know it's your Tady,
    asthore.
Put yo'r lips to the glass till you find it is warmin',
  And I'll thry the outside, though it's frozen all o'er.

Sure, you needn't be shy, for you know I adore you,
  And am now on my way to my cot in the glin,
And but called for to make a short station before you,
  'Till I'm able, mavourneen, to see you agin.

Oh ! good-night ! for the pane's almost meltin', my
    darlin'.
  Oh ! good-night ! for I'm faint ; but to sthrinthen my
    narves,
I'll just call on my way and see ould Paddy Carlin,
  And give his son Tom what I think he desarves.

BIDDY MAGUIRE.

Now, I don't care for murther as long as it's fair ;
But the way that I'm slaughtered 's a sin and a shame ;
For I'm sthrangled all day wid a rope of black hair,
And I'm roasted all night before lips hot as flame.

And I'm riddled wid eyes that are rale shootin' stars,
And that wing me regardless of time or of place ;
While my poor, broken heart is dhragged out through its
    bars,
By a set of white teeth, and shook clane in my face.

But the divil a sthroke can I give in return,
I'm so wake and so dizzy whene'er I go nigh her ;
So, here, durin' life, I may swing, twist and burn,
For it's all. the same thing to that Biddy Maguire.

When she's framed in the door-way, that's opposite
    ours,
Throth, you'd think some ould masther had painted the
    air,
And had ground up the sky and the stars and the
    flowers,
Just to give the last touch to a picther so fair.

But bad cess to the paintin' is in it at all,
But a beautiful craytshure, as meltin' as fire,
'That would butcher your sowl, like a calf in a stall ;
With her innocent looks—That same Biddy Maguire.

Faith I'll give up moon-walkin' and take to my tay,
For I find that I'm nothin' but skin and but bone,
While my neck's got so stretch'd lookin' over the way,
It's the lenth of a gandher's, and not like my own.

Or I'll walk right up to her, without bein' shy,
And show how I'm gone, if I was to expire,
And I'll say to her teeth, if her mother was by,
"Isn't this purty work for you, Biddy Maguire ?"

ASINUS AD LYRAM!

" Critics are already made. "—BYRON.

HE has dropt his pick and shovel, and peeled off his
    grimy dress,
  And has scrubbed himself with soap-suds in a tub ;
For the fellow has decided to go right into the press,
  And pick up a critic's bowie-knife or club.

He knows that education and experience are all stuff,
  And that genius, taste and talent never pay,
And that hosts of interlopers who but swagger, lie and
    puff,
  Cut a figure in the fourth estate to-day.

There is nothing in the way, for he has learned to read
    and write,
  And can plagiarize and bully like the rest ;
And, besides, he knows whatever he may happen to
    indite,
  Is as likely to be paid for as the best.

So he walks into free lunches and some other fellow's
     beer,
  And some fancy words from '' Webster," when he can,
And hangs round a police court, with a pen behind his
     ear ;
  And, lo ! he is a literary man !

And when, through a cracked skylight, or beside a '' tal-
     low-dip,"
  He has studied squibs and play-bills night and day,
And has got some slangy platitudes upon his vulgar lip,
  He is ready and is panting for the fray.

So he struts into the play, where he had never been be-
     fore,
  And the opera, that so blinds him with its glare,
And trampling on the actors, on the singers and the
     score,
  He stands forth a finished critic, then and there !

INO AND BACCHUS.

In an old number of the 'London Art Journal' there is a fine en-
graving from a beautiful group in marble, by Foley, in which Ino and
her infant charge are seen reclining upon the flowery sward; the for-
mer raised on her elbow and turned on one of her hips, while dang-
ling a bunch of grapes over the pouting lips of the rosy god, who
pushes it aside, as if to make for one of her breasts, which is exquisitely depicted.

STANZAS.

One breast was bare, and its nipple lay
Like a crimson star in the milky way ;
　　Shedding round it a soft, pale roseate light
That melted away into dazzling white
　　Shot with veins, of a delicate azure tinge,
That were lost near her shoulder's shining hinge.

Through the pink and pearly charm of her mouth
Her breath came forth on the wings of the South ;
　　While, resting on one of her dimpled hips,
She dangled the grapes o'er the youngster's lips,
　　Who pushed them aside, with a joyous scream,
Preferring his strawberries smothered in cream.

THE DEVOTEE.

From the Irish Anthology.

If those teeth were but bades, Peggy Rooney, asthore,
  I'd go smack at my " duty " by night and by day,
And the flashin' white rosary tell o'er and o'er,
In, I'm sure, what you'd call a most beautiful way.

Wid your dark dhramy eyes as the lamps of my shrine,
  Throwin' light on my upturned face unawares,
And your daisy-tipped lips for a small taste of wine,
If I got, you persave, rather wake at my prayers.

Then, begorra, I think I'd be able to do,
  And repate pather-nosthers and aves galore ;
For, the dickens a bit, but, betune me and you,
  If I'd ax to get up to my legs any more.

And, if even the priesht of the parish they'd bring
  Just to rate me and bid me give over the case,
'Pon my conscience, I tell you I'd do no such thing ;
  Is it give him a chance to pop down in my place ?

BOSTON TEA-PARTY NO. 2.

How consistent the promptings of Boston must be,
When she once more invites the *Atlantic* to tea ;
For although it is many and many a day
Since she had her first fling at Souchong in this way,
The news has just reached us, through tongue and
   through pen,
That her Mohawks have had a tea-party again.

But how different the cup she once brewed on her coast
From the one now decocted to wet her *dry toast*,
For the strength and bouquet of the beverage had then
Laid right hold on the lips and the noses of men ;
But her waves smack no more of the primitive stuff,
The *Atlantic* being now wishy-washy enough.

And, besides, her late guests had been scarce half regaled,
When, from some cause or other, her canister failed,
And, good lack ! she was forced her Bohea to eke out
With some few laurel leaves that lay scattered about.
Upon which her grave teapot so fumed, tossed and
   pitched,
That her Puritan instincts declared it bewitched.

But to some subtler fancies the mystical din,
Filled with snatches of echoes, cried forth from within :
" Come !—Flash out a stream—Hip ! Hurrah !—muffled
        drums—
That child is not mine !—What?—The Frost Spirit
        comes !—
Put him out !—Hail Columbia !—What ?—Not even beer?
Tea and toast !   Let us go, boys!   We're long enough
        here ! "

Only two inspirations of earth are divine—
The one flows from woman, the other from wine ;
And he is of dwarfed intellectual growth
Who refuses to pay proper homage to both,
Or who, in his pettiness ventures to boast
That the one's found in tea and the other in toast.

AN EASY LESSON IN HUMOR AND VERSIFI-
CATION.

A FAT, old, canting English beau once got a berth at
    sea,
To teach us poor, blind Yankee salts, and pocket a
    snug FEE;
Among the sad white-choker chaps they called him
    " Brother JEE."
Which shows the FEE JEE Islands should have been his
    destiny.

And when our *bark* left the last *bight* behind in a fresh
    gale,
And *stood* out under *studdin'*-sails, he soon began to
    RAIL,
And looked as *green*, as though he felt without the
    church's PALE,
While all the RAIL, PALE stingo that he swigged was
    no avail.

Then we *bet* he'd be no *better* till he ceased to yawn and
  stretch,
And knew though he was very *short*, a *long* way he
  might KETCH ;
In fact, he could have scarce looked worse if he were
  a dog's FETCH,
  Nor could a WRETCH FETCH a more dismal phiz before
  Jack Ketch.

But when the *wind reined* in its strength, he rose from
  off his seat,
And frizzed his locks ; though *fat* we saw him *lean* toward being NEAT.
He called the *skipper's* neice "The *cheese*," when he
  got through the FEAT,
As with some NEAT FEET broth she came so smilingly
  and sweet.

And now whene'er our *snoring* craft *slept* in her wake
  once more.
He'd join a boat, *crow* o'er the *crew* , and volunteer a
  ROW'R ;
But if a "cat's paw" touched his faith, he'd tremble at
  the OAR,
And make us ROAR o'ER half the fine, fresh-water creeds
  ashore.

But soon a storm came swooping down the hollows of
    the night,
Through frowning watery citadels, rocked on their
    gloomy SITE ;
While thunders from their battlements cried out, "Man's
    but a MITE ! "
Till such a SIGHT MIGHT well appal the stoutest with
    afright.

Then looked aghast our heavenly guide, though not a
    prayer he told ;
But, *egged* by fear he raised a *hatch* and leaped into
    the HOLD.
When one brave *tar* sung in full *pitch*, as through the
    surge we BOWLED :
"Lay HOLD, BOLD lads ! "   " Amen's the word, but let's
    keep out the cold."

When morning came, to *heal* our grief, the *Asp* took us
    in *tow*,
But fearing *Jee* was lost in *wo*, we all went down to
    KNOW ;
We found him with his *left* leg *right*, but *right* leg *left*
    a BOW ;
So that NO BEAU or sailor has he played since that great
    blow.

EARLY JOYS.

The man who weeps o'er early joys,
   Must be a simple hearted fool;
And can't have gone, like other boys,
   For twelve or thirteen years, to school;

Or felt the daily misery
   Of peeping through the bolted gate,
While some Bob Smith, with savage glee,
   Roars from within, "Tom Jones, you're late!"

What bliss!—to quake our youth away
   At crazy desks, from nine till four,
Or to be caught ten times a day,
   At "Jack and Jill," behind the door.

Or severed almost piece from piece
   For pinching an ill-natured mate
Who bawled out "playing fox and geese."
   Or, "making ladies on a slate."

EARLY JOYS.

How sad to see such senseless toys
   Clasped by a gray-haired youth, in tears,
Unknown to the sublimer joys
   That should attend our graver years.

How sad to know his leaden feet,
   The paths of Truth have never trod,
Nor borne him through their blest retreat,
   One single step towards his God.

KATE ROONEY.

KATE ROONEY.

THERE's not an angel wings the skies
Possesses such a pair of eyes
    As yours, Kate Rooney ;
And as I'm looking at them now,
Starrin' the hivens of your brow,
    I feel quite spooney,

And thravelin' downwards to your lips,
It makes my own as dhry as chips,
    Just wid warm thinkin',
That I would like to taste their dew,
Wid no one by but me and you,
    To watch the dhrinkin'.

HUNTED DOWN.

But I am the unhappy man
    From night till morn—from morn till night ;
For, do the very best I can,
    That cursed best is never right.

Whether I eat or drink or dance,
    Or speak or bow to those who pass,
Or sing or drive, by some mischance,
    I always make myself an ass.

The other day when at a *fête*—
    A splendid *fête* not far from town—
With beating heart, I chanced to meet
    One Mary Anna Julia Brown.

I saw her eyes swore love to mine—
    Such love as words can ne'er express ;
But handing her a little wine
    I spilled it o'er her satin dress !

She smiled, and asked me for some snipe—
   I didn't like that smile !—not I !—
I tried to carve, but such a wipe
   As then I gave her in the eye !

For oh !—the like has ne'er been heard—
   My fork—and I in such a state—
It slipped !—and the accursèd bird
   Flew at her off the cursèd plate.

Oh ! then I shuddered in despair—
   She met me with so dark a frown—
And sinking down into my chair,
   Lost Mary Anna Julia Brown !

I tried to dance some, after that,
   But dancing now was but a bore ;
Yet still I managed to lay flat
   My furious host upon the floor !

But, after all, I sang with grace ;
   And soon, commencing, with a sigh,
I towards the ceiling turned my face,
   But plaster fell into my eye !

Enough !   I rushed from such a fate ;
  And drove off with a deadly groan ;
But oh ! my gig, when at my gate,
  Upset, and broke my collar-bone !

And here, as now I lie in bed,
  A Bachelor, though wed to woe,
I hear, though I can't lift my head,
  My servants drawing corks below !

Then am I not a haunted man
  From night till morn, from morn till night?
For do the very best I can,
  That cursed best is never right !

MICK GRADY.

If I could, throth I'd hop into one iv thim cars,
   And be off, like a shot, up yon glittherin' height,
Just to bring you down lashins and lavins ov stars
   To encircle that neck and that forehead this night.

Don't you see where a river ov light seems to sthray,
   Where the beautiful azure appears to be riven ?
Och ! I'd dash into that, and take bagfuls away,
   For they say that's a mine ov those jewels ov Heaven.

Arrah, may be you think I'd prove false on the road,
   If I step'd into Vesta or Juno or Ceres ;
And that I'd be apt to soon scatther my load
   Amongst their cowld phantoms ov Judies and Marys.

Is it me ? Bluran ounthers ! its you that well know
  That I've no earthly raison to live in the skies,
Whin I've got purer blue and more light here below
  In my own darlin' Molly Mallowney's two eyes;

And, dhin, do you b'lieve I'm a ghost ov a man
  That would spind all his life wid a vaporish lady ?
Throth I'll have somethin' solider, dear, if I can ;
  Cock thim up, to be sure, wid the likes ov Mick Grady !

HINT FOR JANUARY.

IF you want to get warrem, go out in the cowld,
  Wid a pair of young horses that's used to the snow,
And some one by your side you'll be forced for to
    howld,
  On pretinse that the back of the cutther's too low—

Some one upon whom the frost saizes in haste,
  And whose lips are so sure to resaive its first touch,
Though wid keeping them thawed, while supportin' her
    waist,
  'Pon me sowkins the weather won't throuble her much.

And while sheltherin' her thus over valley and hill
  If she says she's so warrem she can't dhraw her
    breath,
"Oh! My God" sez you—hugging her closer up still—
  " People always thinks that whin they're freezin' to
    death !"

RETALIATION.

WHEN the sides of old Time seemed nigh ready to
    crack,
  As he pelted us, laughing, through boyhood together,
With pebble-like moments that dropt in the sack
  That then swung at our shoulders as light as a
    feather ;

Ah ! how little we thought, when just loosed, on the
    road,
  From the frail apron-strings of a kind-hearted mother,
That the villain was tricking us into a load
  That should press on us heavily one day or other.

But, now, since at last we are up to the hoax,
  Let us try to repay the old rogue on the treble,
And pelt him with pipes, empty bottles, and jokes,
  When we find that he's stooping to pick up a pebble.

MATRIMONY.

THE clothes-line over which the poor Kilkenny cats are
   thrown ;
The cage that keeps strange monkeys to the scratch ;
The rope that to the drowning dog securely hangs the
   stone ;
The torch that's always burning near the thatch ;

The thorn that's stuck secure in almost every booby's
   side ;
The wedge that severs those who once were friends ;
The whipping-post to which a woman's earthly joys
   are tied ;
The daily " round and round " that never ends.

The Christian chemistry that blends the water with the
    oil ;
The spoon that's ever emptying out the seas ;
The Joshua that lengthens out the sun of bitter toil ;
The web that joins two rabid Siamese.

The empty space that bulges in the middle of the bed ;
The fly that's always lighting on your nose ;
Things more unlike to matrimony never could be
    said—
As everybody's certain,—I suppose !

THE RAINBOW.

Oh ! how I chafe whene'er I hear those ballad-mongers
    sing
Of the wedding link that binds the golden sunshine to
    the showers ;
Which of them has ever christened it the skipping-rope
    of Spring,
Or the handle of the landscape's balmy basket full of
    flowers ?

Which of them has ever fancied it a swing on yonder
    plain,
Just inverted, by some frolicsome celestials in their
    mirth,
With a swoop that had upset the blessed angel of the
    rain,
Till his stock of liquid jewelry came tumbling to the
    earth ?—

Or believed it but the engine-hose stretched o'er the
    sultry sky ;
Or the bell-rope pulled by nature when she wants to
    wash her face ;
Or the clothes-line upon which the dripping clouds
    are hung to dry ;
Or a thousand other names that I can't mention in
    this place?

Oh how I hate to hear those sorry ballad-mongers
    sing,
Of the gold and purple comb, with all its showery
    silver teeth,
That among the emerald tresses of the beautiful young
    Spring,
Pins the violet and the primrose and the daisy in one
    wreath.

ONE OF THE REASONS WHY.

Wid her piggen on her head,
Comin' up the scinted lane,
Blur and turf !—sure sich a thread
Niver had the Queen of Spain.

Brathin' like a hawthorn bush
Whin in the May-tide morn it blows;
Warblin' like a summer thrush
Whin the day 's about to close.

Light within her faithful heart;
Light within her purple eyes;
Not the soulless light of art,
But the light that niver dies.

Light upon her rounded arms—
On her face and dazzlin' throat ;
Light surroundin' all her charms ;
Till they in a halo float ;

And she's thrue as she is fair—
Thrue as ever prayed to God !
For she'd die a marthyr there
Ere she'd bethray her native sod.

And there's not amongst us one
Who feels not, 'tis for such as she
That now he girds his armor on,
And swears that Ireland shall be free !

KITTY LYNCH.

Oh ! then, cushla machree, I'm just sthruck of a hape,
At the thoughts of the goold you might put in one's purse;
For it's only yourself that can dhress half so chape
Without lookin', mavourneen, a thrawnien the worse.

'Though I'm often beside you—whatever's the cause—
Till this minute I never persaved you were dhrest
In that coorse woollen gown, and that bit of plain gawze
That was white 'till you gave it the lie on your breast.

They may talk of their coortiers that make people stare
Wid their fine silks and sattins so squeezinly laced,
But you'd see how they'd look, in the home-spun, you
      wear,
Wid no more than that runnin'-sthring circlin' their waist.

They may boast of their dainties, their dhrinks, and that
    same,
And dhrive out for a walk in their coaches and four ;
But what can bate sthrawberries smothered in crame,
And a sthroll down the boreen wid——no one, asthore?

Aye, a sthroll that would fill your young heart wid de-
    light,
Till in dhrames—that a saint might be sharin' wid you—
You'd be brathin' the white-thawren hedge the whole
    night,
And be dhrippin' all over wid starlight and dew.

And whin from your mouth some more feverish joy
Sipped the pure liquid balm, as the eager bee sips,
Ten to one but you'd call, unawares, for some boy
Just to dhrop in, a moment, and moisten your lips.

PADDY BLAKE'S "PINNANCE."

Ah ! then take down that image that hangs near the
    althar,
  Or else all my pinnance is useless to me ;
For whin I'm forninst it I'm sure for to falther :
  And its sinnin' I am, Father Luke, do you see !

Put me up some ould saint that is wrinkled and hairy,
  And it's then I'll get through wid my rounds like a
    man ;
But if you let anythin' near me called, Mary,
  'Pon my conshins I'm done for and cannot get an.

Is it "why" that you're roarin' ?—now listen to raison,
  I've a namesake of hers, only barrin' the child,
But that will come right, plaze the Lord, in due saison !
  Arrah ! now Father Luke, don't be gettin' so wild !

Oh ! you'll "add one more saint, shrine and lamp to the
　　canon ! "
　So you say, " till I wear out my knees to the bone !"
Don't be hard ! Add the moon and the banks of the
　　Shannon !
　And begorra ! I'll furnish a saint of my own !

IMPROMPTU.

(On seeing the Balloon " Europa ", made of Irish linen, just ascend at Toronto, Canada, to a great height, on its way to Boston.)

WHY ! In commerce, ould Ireland, I'm glad you're be-
    ginnin'
Just to hould up your head, and to " never say die,"
For, begorra, I'm sure that your beautiful linen
Never went off before, half so quick or so high.

Oh I thin, won't they be glad, from Coleraine up to
    Kerry,
At its rapid and most unaccountable *sale* ?
And, machree, it's no wonder they all should be merry,
For to see that so much can be done by the *Gael.*

MISPLACED CONFIDENCE.

A SKETCH, IN PATENT IAMBICS

As fierce a blast as e're old Boreas blew
    Was piling up the snow-drifts tier on tier,
When from dull Dolly Varden's eyes of blue,
    As through the waste she trudged, fell tear on tear.

Upon her checks and ears, and small snub nose
    The frost had seized relentlessly—poor maid !
And now, but all too late, alas ! she knows
    How stupid the mistake that she had made.

Her hands, the color of a half-boiled beet,
    Beneath her shawl she tries in vain to hide
From gusts that now so wildly on her beat,
    Though all was calm when first from home she hied.

And notwithstanding she was stout and hale,
    The cold had often caused her so much pain,
She always shuddered when the snow or hail
    Began to patter on her window-pane.

But, though at dawn so low the gray clouds rode
    As to presage the day would turn out so,
And that the storm would catch her on the road,
    Should she start off for her Aunt Jane's, to sew,

She heeded not the dull sky's threatening red,
    That pointed plainly to this bitter fare,
Because, she in a morning paper read :
    " The weather will to-day be warm and fair."

KITTY FITZGIBBON.

Charmin' Kitty Fitzgibbon sat inside the doore,
    And, begorra, I b'lieve she was knittin,
Till a moonbame she spied playin' thricks on the flure,
    Quite convaynient to where she was sittin'.

There it danced at her feet, in clear, silvery waves,
    Where some frolicsome shadows were sinjin ;
For it sthramed through the windee, mixed up wid some laves
    That the red goold of autumn was tingin'.

And now, as it fell from the pure, starry skies,
    And consaled in the shade its soft flashes,
It appeared like the light of her own liquid eyes
    Crouched within the dark lair of their lashes.

And she thought, as she gazed on the quiverin' bame,
  That herself was the one could dissimble,
For she felt that if young Paddy Casey then came,
  That she wouldn't be in such a thrimble.

And besides that, she said, while she looked very coy,
  Though her cheeks glowed as red red ribbon,
"Sure it's nothin' to me, for I scarce know the boy,"
  So she did—a' came Kitty Fitzgibbon.

But one half of her face was brought out by the light ;
  And 'twas well that the moon had discretion,
For to give one the whole, would be murther outright,
  And be awkward when caught at "confession."

Although fit for an althar-piece, just as she was,
  'Twould be ticklish, I'm sure, to adore her ;
For when goin' your "rounds" you'd be likely to pause
  Somethin' longer than dacent before her.

But now a light footstep draws rapidly near,
  And she hears but her heart and it only ;
Till a full, mellow voice, whispers low in her ear,
  " Kitty darlin', I thought you'd be lonely."

Then, wilder she thrimbled than thrimbled the light ;
  As she said that she thought 'twas her mother ;
And murmured, half out, that 'twas now afther night,
  And they didn't know much of aich other.

But sthrange ! after sittin' an hour by her side,
  While his tongue flowed in sthrains rich and racy,
When he got up to go, she unconsciously cried,
  "Ah ! then, sure it's not late, Mr. Casey."

SEQUENTIAL.*

On reading a portion of Dr. Oliver Wendell Holmes' letter to a
lady, in which he refers incidentally to his " failing eyes and aching
wrist."

Well, what of it ?   What would you we should under-
    stand ?
It's in logical sequence, most men will insist
That when all the wide world has been shaking your
    hand,
You may fairly expect an odd twinge of the wrist.

And besides, there are those who most plainly avow
That to them 'tis a matter of utter surprise
That the dazzling effulgence that circles your brow
Had not long since most seriously damaged your eyes.

* See appendix (*e*) for Dr. Holmes' letter.

And, what's more, I am sure they would say to your
    face—
And it would not be easy to prove they were wrong—
That they wonder, considering the facts of the case,
How your eyes and your wrist came to hold out so
    long.

But what though your eyes were now closing in night;
And those musical fingers had ceased to inspire?
It would be but to ope to more exquisite light—
It would be but to sweep a more eloquent lyre.

Yet, on this latter point I can't say I'm quite clear,
For should Atropos once catch your magical song,
She might order, whatever was left behind here
That you take your old harp and old fingers along.

TO BELVA L——.

Now Belva, don't be stuck up in that way,
We know you all were only prigged from Adam,
When he in that mysterious slumber lay,
And, hence, that only second-hand your clay,
A fact you dare not venture to gainsay,
For you have downright Scripture for it, madam.

He got his first dig in the ribs we know
On your account, for so the thing is written :
And though it may be very long ago,
We have not yet recovered from the blow,
And scarcely like to take you into Co.
Lest we again should be severely smitten.

But, Belva, on what ever tack you run
I'll stand beside you, and shall never weary ;
And guide you as Apollo guides the sun,
From early dawn until the day is done.—
Nor rest until the petticoats have won—
Let me be your Apollo, Belva dearie.

AN ASPIRATION.

If in Art we're constrained to get rid of the nude,
And to dress our mythology up like a guy,
For heaven's sake, let us get rid of the dude.
That's a thing more offensive by far to the eye.

'Though I think it's too late in the day, I confess,
To make all our Venuses over anew—
What sculptor would work, like a tailor, on dress,
Nor ever again on a classical view?

Let the prude wear smoked glasses, nor ply any more
Her keen, morbid microscope, as she has done.
She need not disturb her chill heart to the core
By a glimpse of some faint, little spot on the sun.

But if we must white-wash our Art, like a wall,
And get into a strict shawl and petticoat mood,
Whatever our marbles or paintings befall,
For heaven's sake, let us get rid of the dude.

NOT AN ORIGINAL.

Yes : woman's a copy, I vow,
  No original, surely, is she;
'Though lovely and all as she's now,
  That she's borrowed, the simplest may see.

For instance, her lips and her eyes
  Where pilfered from, do you suppose?
The one from the blue starry skies,
  The other, 'tis plain, from the rose.

And what of her breath's spicy gale?
  Is it not of the sweet morning breeze,
Coming up from the flowers of the vale
  That bloom at the feet of the trees?

And what of her teeth and her hair?
  'Tis apparent to you and to me,
One's the blackest of night in its lair,
  The other the pearls of the sea.

And her voice is the song of the streams
   That out through the flowery wilds rove ;
And her limbs are the rounded moonbeams,
   That fall though the chinks of the grove.

Yes : woman's a copy, I vow,
   No original, surely, is she ;
'Though lovely and all as she's now,
   That she's borrowed, the simplest may see.

APPENDIX.

(*a*)

CAMBRIDGE, *May* 27, 1879.

MY DEAR SIR :

I HAVE seldom if ever received a more graceful compliment than the lines you sent me of March 3.

Only illness has prevented me from sooner writing to thank you. I beg you to pardon the delay and the seeming negligence on my part in acknowledging those friendly words.

Quite apart from any reference to myself, I think your poem beautiful.

I thank you, and am, my dear Sir,

Very truly yours,

HENRY W. LONGFELLOW.

(*b*)

BOSTON, *May* 24, 1866.

MY DEAR SIR :

I HAVE read your letter and the accompanying verses with interest and pleasure. I find them fluent, graceful, fanciful ; showing as I should think a good deal of practice too as a poetical artist.

I shall hand them, letter and verses, to Mr. James T. Fields of the firm Ticknor & Fields, recommending them to his careful consideration * * *

Believe me, my dear Sir,

Very truly yours,

O. W. HOLMES.

323

(c)

BEVERLY FARMS, *Sept.* 2, 1885.

MANY thanks, my dear Sir, for your kind remembrance, and especially for your very pleasing sonnet, which I have read with much gratification.

Believe me, my dear Sir,

Very truly yours,
OLIVER WENDELL HOLMES.

————

(d)

BOSTON, *Nov.* 29, 1863.

DEAR SIR:

I HAVE read your letter and the accompanying poem with care and interest * * * * I find this poem of yours, delicate, melodious, graceful, well wrought, perhaps a little over fanciful in following out the image of the flaming Treasurer. I shall send it with your letter to Mr. James T. Fields of the firm Ticknor & Fields, publishers of this city. * * *

I am, very truly yours,
O. W. HOLMES.

————

(e)

BOSTON, *April* 23, 1888.

MY DEAR SIR:

I AM very thankful that I have sight and strength of wrist enough to write with my own hand, and thank you for your lively, graceful and inspiriting verses. I am grateful for such a pleasant compliment.

Believe me, my dear Sir,

Very truly yours,
OLIVER WENDELL HOLMES.

(*ſ*)

BOSTON, *Dec.* 30, 1870.

I THANK you heartily for your spirited lines recalling the old Christmas. As I look out here from my new home on the wintry landscape, the picture of the old hall and the yule log and the wassail bowl, brings back all my romantic associations with the old festival which again give way to the better realities of

" The land of the river, the cedar and pine,"

and call up visions of happy faces, and cheerful homes throughout all its length and breadth; for I hope there is hardly any part of it where the Christian anniversary did not find something of comfort and enjoyment.

And so with renewed thanks I wish you at least the remembrance of a happy Christmas and the pleasure of a great many such in the future.

Very truly yours,

O. W. HOLMES